To the Last
Man I Slept with

and All the Jerks Just Like Him

To the Last Man I Slept with

and All the Jerks Just Like Him

By

gwendolyn Zepeda

Arte Público Press
Houston, Texas

This volume is made possible through the City of Houston through The Cultural Arts Council of Houston, Harris County.

Recovering the past, creating the future

Arte Público Press
University of Houston
452 Cullen Performance Hall
Houston, Texas 77204-2004

Cover design by Giovanni Mora.
Cover art by John M. Valadez, "Adam and Eva, The Guest is Leaving," 1986.

Zepeda, Gwendolyn
    To the Last Man I Slept with and All the Jerks Just Like Him / by Gwendolyn Zepeda
      p. cm.
    ISBN 1-55885-406-1 (trade pbk. : alk. paper)
      I. United States—Social life and customs—Fiction. I. Title.
    PS3626.E46T6   2004
    813'.6—dc22   2004048531
                                                                    CIP

♾ The paper used in this publication meets the requirements of the American National Standard for Information Sciences—Permanence of Paper for Printed Library Materials, ANSI Z39.48-1984.

4 5 6 7 8 9 0 1 2 3   10 9 8 7 6 5 4 3 2 1

Contents

Low Brow

Fiction Is Good Because It Lets You Pretend You're Lying

For Aunt Sylvia.

Half-White Child of Hippies, Born in Houston in 1971

I Hate Clowns

*E*very time I tell this story, it's different. I've told it so many times, by now it's probably a lie. But it lives in me like a fungus, and I have to vomit out as much of it as I can, whenever I get the chance.

When I was little, my parents got divorced and my mother went to live in a hospital. My brothers and I lived with my father. I love my dad very much, but he didn't know how to dress us right. We dressed ourselves and our clothes never matched. My dad sometimes forgot to cut our nails or to make sure that we used the shampoo and not the conditioner when we were taking a bath. But it was okay. He loved us, he taught us many important things, and he took us to the mall.

One day there was a clown making balloon animals in one of the mall's hallways. The mallway. Whatever. The clown was just like every other clown I've ever seen in Texas—an older white guy dressed in polka dots and big shoes. He had black stubble showing under his red nose and white makeup. All around him there were little blond children laughing and screaming for balloon animals. Their thin blond mothers waited impatiently around them. My brothers told my dad they wanted balloon animals. I wanted a balloon animal, too, but I already knew, even though I was only eight, that this was going to be a bad scene.

My dad went to sit on a bench, where he pulled a science

fiction paperback out of his back pocket and began to read. We waited around the clown for our turn. I tried not to stare at the little blond children and their thin blond mothers. I remember reflexively making my hands into fists so that no one would see my nails. I couldn't hide the fact that I was wearing boy's corduroys with a hole in the knee, or that my hair was tangled around cheap plastic barrettes from Fiesta instead of barrettes with beads and ribbons made by a thin blond mother, but I could hide my dirty nails. I remember looking at my little brothers' hands and wishing they would make them into fists, too. But they were too far away for me to whisper it to them.

As the clown made each balloon animal, he would crack jokes. After a while, even though I was only seven or eight at the most, I realized that most of his jokes were of a personal nature. He would say to a little boy, "Hey, pardner, I like your boots. You gonna be roping some cattle today?" All the other kids would laugh.

The clown would say to a little shampoo-commercial-looking girl, "Boy, you sure are pretty. Who are you, Marilyn Monroe?" And the kids would laugh some more, as if they knew who in the hell Marilyn Monroe was. While we waited, I became more and more nervous. I knew the clown was going to say something about me, and I didn't think it was going to be that I was pretty.

When my brother got to the front of the line, he started excitedly telling the clown what kind of animal he wanted. But the clown had to crack his joke, first. He looked right down at my brother's hands—it was like he had read my mind—and said, "Boy, you sure gotta lotta dirt in those nails. Whaddaya do, grow potatoes in 'em?"

Everyone laughed. At first my brother did too, but as the bratty little bastards laughed harder, pointing at his fingernails and screaming "Ha, ha—ha, ha, ha!" he realized what was going on and put on his blank face.

My brothers and I all had our blank faces. They were the ones we wore when sincere white women asked, "Where is your mother?" and we, sincerely, couldn't tell them where our thin white mother was. They were the ones we wore when the bright blond people with their shiny clean nails looked at my father and whispered, "Is he one of those *Iranians?*" "No . . . I think he's a *wetback.*" Although I was only seven or eight, I had already learned to use my blank face all the time. I tried to set the example for my brothers, but they were still too young to understand the way life was.

The clown, who was probably an alcoholic who couldn't keep a better job, paused so that all the laughter could subside. Then he said, "You know, sometimes a little soap and water can be your best friend." The brats and their mothers nodded solemnly, recalling the verse from their Middle-White-People Class Bibles.

As the clown finished up his inflated masterpiece, I ground my teeth and imagined how sweet life would be when I grew up and got rich. I would drive to the mall in my Stingray Corvette. I would walk inside, wearing my tall brown boots and flowing skirt like the ladies from Fleetwood Mac. I would point to the clown with a long, clean fingernail and say, "*You are stupid.*" He would immediately remember what he had done to my brother and, seeing how rich and beautiful I had become, would feel very, very sorry. Maybe he would even die.

The clown made my youngest brother a balloon without comment, and then I dragged both brothers away to the bench where my father was waiting. He looked up from his book and asked where my balloon was. I told him I was too old for those things, and then we went home.

I thought about becoming a professional clown killer after I graduated from high school. But then, instead, I went to college.

Blue Birds

I went to Kindergarten at A small neighborhood school right near the center of Houston. Our class consisted of children of Mexican immigrants, children of Vietnamese immigrants, and me, a half-white child of hippies who had been plunged, through tragic circumstance, into the barrio of her Chicano father's extended family.

Our school planned to put on a program for the parents. It would consist of musical performances and important information about new teachers, student accomplishments, and head lice epidemics. My class—the Kindergarten class—was to dance to a song about birds. The choreography rehearsals were intense. We formed a circle with our clasped hands and then, one by one, each student would play the part of the happy bird that flew around that circle, weaving in and out under the raised wings of its peers. Although we did this in time to a jaunty piano tune with optimistic lyrics, the only looks I remember on our faces were those of confusion, apathy, or grim five-year-old determination.

A week or so before the big event, our teacher Mrs. Miles mimeographed notes detailing what we were to wear on the day of the program, and pinned them to our shirts so that we could courier them to our families. My note was a page-length drawing of a girl in a long skirt and blouse. It very clearly said (in English, at least) that the skirt was to be

6

blue and the blouse was to be red. The boys had only to wear white shirts and black pants, in keeping with American men's formalwear customs of the last several hundred years.

My grandmother, the matriarch of our house, put on her glasses and studied the note, then conferred with my father and my aunt. Some time after that, a small red skirt and blue blouse were posted on a coat hanger, high on the closet door.

I knew that it was all wrong. I knew that it was supposed to be a *blue* skirt and a *red* blouse—it said so right there on the note. I didn't dare to broach the subject with my grandmother, though, knowing from hard experience that her reply would be something like, "Go over there and look at the note. *Mira*—no, not there, There! Pick it up you think it's gonna bite you? Get your hair out of your face. Look at what it says. How can you be so smart at school and so dumb at home? *Chinelas*. I told your daddy he should have baptized y'all." It would end in me being, as usual, the one who had gotten things wrong.

Carrying out my tradition as class misfit, I walked to school on the day of the program with my hair uncombed and in the wrong clothes. All the other girls in our class had known each other since the day they were born or a couple of weeks before that, in the towns below the Texas border before their parents had risked crossing the Rio Grande in order to give their children the gift of performing in American public school programs. These girls' mothers had all gone to Clothworld together and bought the same red fabric and the same blue fabric, and then gone to each other's houses and sewn all weekend. These girls showed up on the morning of the program with exactly matching red blouses and blue skirts, and red lipstick and blue eye shadow. I was the odd little girl out, deeply ashamed.

Mrs. Miles looked at me pensively for a while and then went across the hall to consult with Mrs. Yee. They were often discussing me, poor motherless child that I was, or else taking turns trying to comb the tangles out of my hair.

It was decided that my fashion faux pas could be played off. I was supposed to read a little speech in the program, anyway, introducing the new music teacher. I had been taken out of class during naptime for two consecutive days in order to practice saying "round of applause" without a stutter. It would seem, it was decided, as if I were purposely dressed in colors exactly opposite from those of my classmates in honor of my two-sentence speech.

The hour of the program arrived. We danced our dance, and I said my speech. Everyone clapped. I felt a little better.

My dad didn't see the program. He hadn't wanted to miss a day of his job with the big typewriter manufacturer that would lay him off within the year and then go on to become a multi-billion-dollar computer corporation. My grandmother wasn't able to attend the program, either— maybe because of important developments in her favored daytime television series.

I never told my family that they had put me in the wrong outfit, or that I'd been chosen to read a speech. But, for the next program, I did ask my aunt to give me some lipstick.

❧≪

At the age of six, one of my goals was to learn to be sexy. Our cousins and babysitters Monica and Biba, although they now deny it, were my most influential mentors in this regard. They had the long hair and tight jeans that I yearned for and that kept their teachers from telling them apart. My brother and I knew the difference, though, having spent many hours with them between elementary school dismissal and my father's rush hour commute. Biba was the fighter with the extra-spicy vocabulary. Monica was the lover with the sophisticated ways. Sixth-grade men left their longtime girlfriends in hopes of catching Monica's eye. When these girlfriends sought vengeance, Biba defended her sister with furious, birthstone-ringed fists. Then, the sisters fought each other with icy taunts, dramatic slamming of doors, and hair pulling extraordinaire.

I aspired to Monica's popularity and Biba's independence. They taught us many, many things: how to make wishes with fallen eyelashes, which cartoons were worth watching, the meaning of the word fag, and how to curve one's knuckles perfectly while throwing the finger.

One year Monica showed us the school portrait in which she stared haughtily into the camera.

"How come you're not smiling?" I asked.

"Because boys think it's sexier when you look mean," she explained.

I mentally filed that away.

The next year, her picture featured crinkled eyes and a dimple on which all the grownups commented favorably.

"How come you're smiling?" I asked when we were alone.

"Because the stupid fucking camera man kept telling me I was sexy," she scowled. I resolved to be on my guard for such things.

Whenever we wished on eyelashes, stars, or slow-moving planes, Biba's wish was to be fifteen. I lived in awe of that age, wondering what the teenager who'd taught me about bras and Kotex could possibly have left to learn.

One afternoon, Monica and Biba taught us to dance. Biba put a disco record on the turntable they'd gotten for Christmas. In the dark little corridor between their bedroom and the bathroom, Monica said, "Look, I'll show y'all The Freak." She danced to the slow throbbing beat. We copied her movements, rocking our tiny pelvises back and forth and running the tips of our fingers from our hips to our heads and back down again. My brother Zonky, in pre-Kindergarten at the time, successfully mimicked Monica's eye-closing and sensual moans.

During the twenty-five years that have elapsed since then, he has done The Freak or variations on that theme with women all around the world. Unable to loosen up enough to win approval that day in the hall, I eventually became a housewife. So did Monica and Biba, actually. I was disappointed, expecting them to end up as game show hostesses or Russian double agents. There's still time, though. I'll give them another couple of years.

ॐ∞

When I was in first grade, I played a secret game with another Spanish-surnamed, white-looking girl whose name was Regina. We would run to the space below the stairs or the corner under the fire escape slide. I would whisper, "Let's speak Spanish!"

She would gesture and toss her hair like her mother as the long vowels and un-aspirated consonants flowed from her mouth. I would hold my hands up as if smoking one of my grandmother's Pall Malls and rasp, "*Bueno . . . éste . . .* mapalapa repalaba catobalabra. *Pos, mira . . .* el quelapraca-pa. *¡Ven p'acá! ¡Ándale!*" One of the few real Spanish words I knew was *bolilla*. It meant "white girl." I never said that during our games.

I went to a different, special school for second grade but saw Regina again years later, in a different, special high school. Unnerved by my new surroundings and relieved to see a former comrade speaking fluent Spanish with her friends, I pulled Regina aside and asked if she remembered me. She said she did.

"Hey, remember we used to pretend to speak Spanish all the time? I finally learned it for real, too!" I proudly confided.

There was a pause and a vague reply. Then she smiled

and gently went away.

It didn't even occur to me until many years later that she had probably been speaking real Spanish from the very beginning.

ᕬᕬ

Still in first grade, I had a fight with a new Spanish-surnamed white-looking girl. (It was the 1970s. Suddenly, they were popping up all over the place.) Peggy and I decided that we didn't like the looks of each other and nothing would remedy the situation more quickly than a fistfight in the schoolyard.

Under the coaching of my cousins and Peggy's big sisters, we managed to complete three rounds of mutual hair pulling before the bell rang and all the spectators deserted us for class. Sweaty and exhilarated from our moment in the ring, Peggy and I became friends.

This relationship filled the recent gap in my social life left by the slow desertion of my best friend, Letty. Although she had, like many of our classmates, newly arrived from Mexico, Letty's love of learning and quick ear for language had made her the only child in our Kindergarten, besides me, who knew the whole alphabet. This mutual exclusivity had forged our friendship. The very next year, however, cut-throat classroom politics erected barriers between us.

"Which one do you like better—red or blue?" asked jealous Idresima as Letty looked on. I picked red, being that it was the color of lipstick and the sports cars driven by the best characters on TV.

"Ha, ha! We like blue because *that's* the color of heaven," she said, fingertips touching and eyes piously rolling upward. "Red's the color of the DEVIL! You're going to HELL!"

I met Letty's eyes silently as everyone around us

laughed. She said nothing.

Exposed as the agnostic liberal my parents had raised, I had no choice but to spend the rest of my recess hours at the school playing with the white children of hippies. They had trickled into our neighborhood as their parents got old and discovered the joys of renovating Victorian homes.

ஃ

In second grade, I went to a school that had a special program for students deemed "gifted and talented." We fed the government's hunger for statistics by filling out forms several times a year. On the line above "RACE," I copied what I had seen my father write many times: Mexican, hyphen, American. Later that would change to a mere check in a box next to "Hispanic," and then a darkened bubble next to "Latino," and then a write-in of "mixed" before, twenty years later, I finally decided it was none of anyone's business. My best friend Fay'El was half-white and half-black, but she adamantly claimed the non-white half of her heritage and taught me to do the same with pride. One of the most popular girls in our grade was half Mexican and half Chinese. Although I felt comfortable with children of all races, I became increasingly aware, through my interactions with our classroom's ethnic majority, that I was not really white.

Now I only had to convince everyone else. We still lived in the same neighborhood. I knew that I now went to a better school than most of the other kids, and that my father made a little more money, and I tried to be gracious about it. I shared my Barbies with girls in the neighborhood. I learned enough Spanish to pay proper respect to their mothers. I walked to the corner store and supported my brothers and the neighborhood boys in their struggles against the video game consoles.

Or maybe, *sometimes,* I wasn't so gracious. Maybe I

learned to show off by saying big words or writing cutesy stories, just like a smart-assed little white girl—pissing off the neighborhood kids but making our white teachers wish they could take me home and buy me candy and barrettes. Maybe only sometimes when I felt like a lonely little loser. I don't remember for certain. It was a long time ago.

My attempts to conform weren't enough to please certain people. María from three blocks away decided she hated me because of the color of my skin. "Hey, *bolilla!*" she'd yell down the street. "Hey, *pinche bolilla!*"

One day I gained the courage to yell back, "I'm not a *bolilla!*"

"What are you then—a nigger?" she screamed laughing.

Overcome by the foreignness of her logic and vulgarity, I turned and ran away.

❧

My submission to puberty brought about a change of status and expectations within my family. At holiday gatherings, I graduated from the games of the front yard to the conversation of the kitchen. I was allowed to perform the most junior of traditional *tamale*-making tasks—the spreading of the *masa*—while listening to the women talk. Sometimes the topic was me and the other examples of burgeoning womanhood in our family.

"Whatever you do, don't marry a Mexican," our cousin Helen, who had married a Mexican, would tell us teenage girls. Her mother and all the others who'd married Mexicans or men of Mexican descent would laugh. Our cousins who'd married white men would laugh. Our cousin Joanne, a white woman who'd married into our mostly Mexican family, would laugh, too.

"Go for the white meat, y'all!" Helen would tell us, while all the women laughed some more. Then, one of the cousins who married a white man was sure to say, "Don't marry a *bolillo*, either. They ain't any goddamned better." And they would all laugh like witches, only pausing to hand a Budweiser to any husband who might poke his head into our kitchen.

❧

The more things changed, the more they stayed the bittersweet same. My fifth-grade class studied Greece for our big Christmas Around the World program. We made crepe paper aprons in yellow, red, and orange to layer over our skirts. The teacher asked if I could bring cookie sheets from home, and I encountered a language barrier. I didn't know what "cookie sheets" were. We made our cookies on "pans" that we bought at the Goodwill or Fiesta Dollar Store. I told the teacher we had no cookie sheets at home, and she looked at me in a weird way. I surreptitiously checked my hair for tangles.

A boy named Kyle told me I looked sexy. I ignored him, frightened by his red hair and freckled skin. I went back to work on my aprons, and the teacher gave me a note. A note to take to my parents.

"White blouse and *brightly colored* skirt," it said. There may have even been specific suggestions—red, orange, yellow, or bright blue. But it didn't really matter what the note said.

I watched my father and his mother hunched over a roll of dark green polyester twill, so dark green it was almost black. They were cutting out a skirt.

When they got to the hem, I don't know if they ran out of dark, dark green thread or if they were just tired, but they decided to fasten it with masking tape. "*Pos*, quit complaining, Gwendolyn. We don't have money to buy things like all the *bolillos* at your school."

Another circle dance. This time we were running, sideways round and round, hands lifted high. I avoided Kyle's gaze, which was steady on my lipstick. The tinny Greek music twanged and something pulled at my foot. Something rasped against the floor, then grabbed and stuck to my leg. I almost tripped over a long wad of dark green threads. My skirt! The masking tape!

I couldn't stop dancing. The multi-colored hands pulled me on and on. I stumbled and prayed not to fall as Kyle leered at me from across the circle. The red and orange and yellow and bright blue skirts flashed before my eyes. I wanted to cry.

But I didn't.

My family hadn't made it to that program, either. Afterwards, my grandmother asked me what in the heck I had done to my skirt. I shrugged and went to my room. Later I would sneak the Whitman's chocolates from her bureau, along with the eye shadows that were yellow, green, and blue. I would look in the mirror and become the sultry dark-haired dancer—the exotic and deadly spy. I would make myself the same promises as always. No one could guess how sexy and powerful I would be when I grew up and went away.

I Used to Steal

*I*t started with a roll of candies. Actually, I'm not even sure they were candies. They were hard square lozenges in dark green wrapping with a fancy font my six-year-old eyes couldn't read. Probably either some imported mints marketed for adult tastes or, worse, just cough drops. They were like sugar plums children dreamed about it in stories they read to us in school. I didn't know what they were, but I knew I was supposed to want them.

My five-year-old brother had shown me how easy it was to put this roll of desire into my pocket. I suspect my mother had shown him before she went away. He had been her favorite, and she never let a lack of cash stop her from getting him what he wanted.

I got as far as the door, but then my nervousness gave me away. My father made me give the candy to the clerk and apologize. My eyes stung with tears and shame. Satisfied with the completion of his duty as a single parent, my father led us out of the store and moved on with his life. He never caught me stealing again.

❧

There wasn't much pleasure in the bubble gums and plastic jewelry I subsequently shoplifted, because the guilt always outweighed it. However, the gradual onset of poverty in our household led to more and more regular thievery of neccessities—food and clothes. Water. Electricity.

I convinced myself that those with money expected it, anyway, and that the thrift stores deserved it for pricing their merchandise higher than their clientele could afford. I never stole from stores where the clerks had been friendly to me, or where the owners were elderly. I believed that a man who stole bread to feed his family wasn't really a criminal. But at the same time, one thing led to another. There were needs I couldn't deny, needs that bread couldn't satisfy.

We used to steal decadence. Not just bread to fill our stomachs, but cream puffs and éclairs to gorge on until we vomited into bus station trash cans.

We used to steal glamour. We carried eye shadows, lip glosses, and magazines to the little alcove in the corner of the store. My brother, now eleven, had figured out all security camera angles. We each turned around and let the other two unzip our backpacks and filled our backpacks with the shiny merchandise and walked away smiling. We didn't stop to watch the cashiers as they made the darker children check their bags at the door.

Cigarettes and wine coolers followed this. A girl had to maintain her image. Unlike my brothers, I never went so far as to steal cars. I didn't know how to drive.

Several years and one miraculous surprise of a full college scholarship later, I left home. I got a job. I was ready to embark upon a new life as a good citizen.

꙳

College life and good citizenship were a complete culture shock. I lived through freshman year as an uneasy spectator until I met a man who shared my vice. We stole together on nights and weekends, obsessing and giggling like it was kinky sex. We moved in together. We pilfered monkey wrenches from Montgomery Wards and wheelbarrows from

Wal-Mart. Strolled into the grocery store wearing winter coats and took lipsticks, batteries, and packages of ham. All the things to make a happy home.

One day, he got arrested. He'd been caught stealing a dress for me from Sears—a dress I'd pointed out to him as appropriate for my new job.

Panicked, I called one of the well-off mentors of my high school years and confessed the whole sordid story. She drove me downtown to bail him out. Then she drove me to a far-away mall parking lot, where we sat in her BMW and talked for an hour about why stealing was wrong. Then she took me into the mall and bought me dresses and blouses and pants, saying that I should have told her I needed work clothes so badly. I was contrite. She never heard about me stealing again.

ᡠᡣ

I put on my work clothes and went to work. I resolved to be good. Then, one day, I went to Walgreens and decided that it was impossible to be good without a French mani-cure. But I couldn't justify the expense of such a luxury. I fingered a box that had the face of a well-off woman. It contained moon-curved stickers and pink and white paint. I tucked the box into the waistband of my skirt. Wouldn't Walgreens be proud to sponsor my success?

College-educated arrogance and lack of practice had made me careless. A tiny device on the end of the box made the sensors near the exit squawk indignanyly as I passed. Everyone in the whole store turned to gawk as I tried to talk my way out of my situation with the cashier. He didn't buy the excuse I made. Having settled on a career at Walgreens, he couldn't comprehend the drive behind them. I was shown no compassion.

A grim, lean woman in a uniform and badge came and dragged me by the arm to the freestanding "security office" two steps above the rest of the floor. I quickly summed up her type from my experience as a supple coed. She looked like the kind of woman who'd take me home and spank me to the rhythm of a loud country western song. I didn't want to wind up in her handcuffs. I didn't want to be the sweet young thing in a trashy movie about women's prison inmates wrestling and glistening. Desparate, I found myself batting my eyes in order to strike a deal.

She made me sign a shadily worded agreement to pay Walgreens $300 over the next year. She made me promise that I'd never enter her store again. I had let her get away with this without even buying me a drink.

I choked down breaths of relief as I stumbled out of the automatic doors and into my car. And then a realization hit me. Paying for things actually had value. Paying for things was a contract—an opportunity to insure yourself against bondage and obligation.

I realized what respectable life was all about: working a boring job all week in order to buy useless things all weekend. That was what it meant to be a *consumer*. Thus was the American way.

Later I'd go back to the Walgreens with a more expensive hair-style, in my respectable corporate outfit and professionally done nails. The security guard would stop me at the entrance and say (firmly but not *too* loud), "Get out of my store." Pushed back but not punched out, I'd go away and work harder. Buy myself more expensive things.

The thrill of acquiring luxury items was the exact same whether I paid for them or not. So was the lack of fulfillment—the false hope of happiness constantly pursued. But that was a lesson I could learn at my leisure without the guardians of the American way manhandling my tender flesh. Without the threat of jail hanging over my hungry head.

Aunt Jeanie

I need some of them copper bracelets for my arthritis. It's acting up real bad. I was taking that Anapracin but I had to quit on account of my heartburn. I think I have an ulcer. I told that to Dr. Rajeem but he didn't do nothing. Those Saudi Arabians have real ugly attitudes sometimes.

Y'all need to come over tomorrow morning and have some *chilaquiles.* I'll make 'em real spicy the way your husband likes them. I know he has to work; just come early. Can you get up early? Boy, I tell you, I'm so tired. I got up at three thirty this morning. I couldn't sleep 'cause I had real bad pains in my chest. A real bad stabbing pain, like the kind your uncle had right before he had his heart attack. I didn't get to sleep 'til one o'clock in the morning. I stayed up late working on the Mary costume for the church pageant. My arthritis was hurting so bad! But I told Father O'Neil three weeks ago I'd do it, and he needed it today, so I had to stay up late to cut it out and sew it.

It came out so pretty. I made it purple with a pink sash. Not light pink—a real pretty, dark one. It came out real good. I took it to the church and I saw the Joseph costume that Lola Flores made. That woman can't even sew. She made it red with a silver lamé belt. I don't think silver lamé looks good, do you? I gotta go to Wal-Mart and get some gold lamé before the pageant tomorrow.

I swear, that Lola Flores thinks she's so good. She had that stupid mutt with her at the church. Father O'Neil tried to pet it and it almost bit his hand off. She said it was sick. You know how she talks: "My little Pepper's not feeling good! I'm gonna take him to the Korean's store and see if they can do some acupuncture on him!"

I hope they get that dog and stick a needle in his eye. Then maybe he'll quit coming over here and eating my Cinnamon's food.

A Big-Breasted Woman Is
a Hard Thing to Be

*W*hen I was a teenager, I had large breasts. Imagine the constant "accidents":

"Oh, excuse me. There's a lot of people on this bus and I brushed against you by accident, young lady."

"Oops—the hallway's real crowded, huh? Don't mind me standing pressed against you with this leer on my face and the eventual erection you might feel against your leg."

"Oh, I beg your pardon, madam. I didn't see your breasts there under the water as I backstroked by and accidentally squeezed one of them in my hand. Do forgive me."

Picture the young male hospital volunteers who kept finding excuses to walk into my room as I nursed my first-born child like a Wal-Mart-clad Madonna. I realized what they were up to, but I just sighed and went on feeding my baby. A roomful of strangers had just seen me open as wide as a woman can be, screaming curse words as I pushed a human being out of the part of me you couldn't pay to view in soft-core porn. If these guys wanted to sneak peeks of my tired breasts leaking colostrum all over the sheets, I didn't really care anymore.

How many stories could there be? So many I forget them and they're replaced and I forget those and they all become a wash—the foundation on which I stand as I strap on my reinforced underwire in the morning. The annoyances and humiliations fade like flowered lace, wear out like the hooks against my back, and I just reach in my drawer for more.

My full-figured Aunt Sylvia told me a story from her youth. She grew up in the days when teenage girls regularly dropped out of eighth grade to take jobs at factories or downtown stores, including a version of Woolworth's where they sold elegant veiled hats and gold watches instead of the condoms and cheap candy they offered when I was a teen. I listened, fascinated, as she told of saving up for the pink, three-dollar bra with extra seams, instead of her usual plain white one for only a dollar. She had ironed the precious pink bra so it would lie smooth under her uniform blouse. Instead, the iron had snapped it into the twin cones that we see in the tongue-in-cheek antique lingerie ad reproductions today. My aunt, with no other brassieres washed or aired for that day, was forced to go to her conveyor belt station with breasts that jutted out like missiles, pointed projectiles almost too sharp for men's eyes. She told me about the one special, kind young man who sometimes spoke to her, and of the narrow-eyed girl who painted her nails red and coveted that man for herself. She told how the mean girl, worldlier than my aunt, called the man over one morning and then asked my teenage aunt to please hop up and down a few times. My aunt—sweet, bosomy, and naïve, with soft brown eyes and billows of curly hair she couldn't control—did as she was told, figuring there must have been a reason. Her boobs bounced. The bitch and all her friends exploded into the musical peals of laughter they probably practiced every night, and my aunt burned with shame, never to speak to the kind young man again.

Even as I listened to that story, myself the same age that my aunt was on that evil day, I was able to understand the ways of the world. I said to her, "But, Aunt Sylvia, he probably liked it when your boobs bounced up and down." Although I was by no means powerful, girls of my generation had been lucky enough to cast off at least half the naiveté. My aunt nodded, but bitterly, remembering opportunity lost.

I imagined her reborn as a sort of superhero, walking around downtown with her pink satin torpedo breasts, wiping out injustice among sisters and causing the good strong men of the town to jerk off all night long.

After a few minutes of that reverie, I remembered that I had to be downtown, myself, to meet classmates at the library. We said goodbye, Aunt Sylvia letting me leave the house with my own missile breasts exploding in the flimsy knit top I had outgrown the summer before. If I fought for anything the rest of that day, it was for the right to walk down the sidewalk in peace.

god

The other day a feminist friend asked me if I really believed in God. I said I did. She said, "But you believe God is a woman, right? Or, at least, that he's half female?"

"No," I said. "I know that God is a man. Otherwise he wouldn't let women go through so much shit."

രൂ

I had to wash the piled-up dishes today. I thought about what I would do if I were suddenly to become God. Let's say God decided to pass the crown and He picked me to succeed Him. (I don't know why He would do that. I didn't get into the logistics of it.)

So I'd be God. At first I was thinking that maybe no one would know the difference.

People would pray to me. Some of the prayers I'd answer immediately, and the others I'd leave in my inbox for later. I'd get to them two months later, or else I'd wait so long that I'd be ashamed to answer the prayers and I'd delete them instead.

"Why doesn't God answer our prayers?" those people would say.

People would suffer. I'd try to alleviate some of the suffering, but then I'd get annoyed that there was so much, and

I'd end up ignoring the bulk of it. "Oh, quit your whining," I'd say. "Aren't you old enough to fix it yourself?" And I'd go off and buy supplies to make a new plant or bacteria or something.

"Why does God allow suffering?" people would say.

❧❧

That's how I thought it would be, at first. But then I knew I was kidding myself—that it wouldn't be that way at all. I realized that my heavenly reign would be decadent, political, and totally selfish, like that of the gods of Mount Olympus.

The first thing I'd do is give all my friends little godships of their own. "I want Veronica to be the Goddess of the Hearth and Long-Distance Phone Conversations," I'd say. And I'd dole out little powers and omniscience and things to them. Then I'd set up a really good meeting place for us all—sort of like Mount Olympus, but warmer and not so high. (Did you think I meant Hell? No. But I am afraid of heights.) We'd sit around and gossip about all our mortals, drink sacred beverages, and stash the tributes we'd raked in.

Then, once all that was set up, the real fun would begin. The temples would be built and people would start worshipping in earnest. And—I'm not gonna lie—I'd binge on some massive slaughter. Goodbye to all the rapists, child molesters, and people who'd done me wrong. Maybe they'd go in a big flood. Maybe in a plague of grasshoppers. I don't know. I don't like to dwell on those things.

The things I'd prefer to dwell on are the details. "This person is humble and thrifty," I'd say. "She will win the Publishers' Clearinghouse Sweepstakes. This person is vain and mean. Her hair will be orange for a year. This person makes me smile. I will visit him in the form of Hello Kitty and he will bear my child."

I'd have fun. I'd throw thunder and lightning or make it rain frogs to get my point across. I'd reassume human form, go down to Earth, and test people. I'd make them prove their love.

But, then again, I'd probably get tired of that after a while and eventually become like the first god I described. I imagine a deity probably gets bored after so many years.

Was that silly and megalomaniacal? It's only something I thought of while washing the dishes.

ghost

You know what would suck? It would suck if you became famous, and then died, and then became a ghost, and then someone made a movie about your life, and the movie sucked. Let's say you're a ghost and you get to go into the theater and see the movie, and you hate it. What could you do? Maybe you'd yell, "That's not even how it happened!" in your ghostly voice, and no one would hear. You could always haunt the theater, I guess, but that wouldn't do much good because they'd be showing the movie all over the country. Maybe all over the world, if you'd been famous enough.

So you'd just be sad. A sad ghost.

If I were a ghost, I would be so damned bored. As a child, I thought that it would be great, hilarious fun to be a ghost. But I now believe that I was wrong.

I thought that I would follow people around and play little pranks on them. What good would that do, though? Let's say I followed my husband around . . . Let's say my husband's an old widower, and I follow him around and break something every time he tries to kiss some other lady. What good would that do? Maybe he'd be afraid to kiss other women, but it's not like he'd say, "That must be the ghost of Gwen punishing me! I vow henceforth to be celibate and put extra fake flowers on her grave!" Even if he did say that, I wouldn't want him to do it.

I thought that I'd float around and eavesdrop on people. I could hear all their secrets and see all their scandals. That wouldn't be worth anything, either, though. What good are secrets and scandals if you can't gossip about them to anyone?

I thought I would appear to people in their dreams and give them little messages. Like what, though?

"Letty, this is Gwen. Tell everyone to put fake flowers on my grave."

"Melissa, this is Gwen. I like that sweater you had on the other day."

"Tad, this is Gwen. I'm still dead."

It just isn't worth the effort. Even if I had some great mystery to help resolve, like Patrick Swayze did in the movie *Ghost*, I wouldn't want to mess with it. Too much trouble for too little return, I say.

Maybe I could catch up on all the movies I missed, though.

I used to think that the best part would be hearing what people said about me after I was gone. Now I realize that it would only upset my ghostly self. I'd listen and then either think, "That's not true! That's not the way it was at all!" or else I'd think, "Yeah, that was true. But what does it matter now?"

So I guess instead of wasting time as a ghost, I'll just go straight to hell.

That's my plan.

Just kidding. I don't believe in any of that crap, anyway.

Raining

*I*t was raining like crazy this morning after a long spell of no daytime rain at all. I don't have an umbrella. I never have one. I never *have* had one. Don't ask me why.

My car was parked 40 or 50 feet from my door and the parking lot was developing a shallow moat. I decided to wait out the worst of it. Checked my email, updated my budget, and it was still raining like a big rain bucket from hell. I halfheartedly searched my apartment for a non-existent umbrella, even though I already knew what I would have to do. I just didn't want to do it.

My late grandmother's translucent head floated over my left shoulder, crabbily telling me, "Just use a trash bag."

But I don't want to use a trash bag, Grandma. I'd rather die. I'd rather wait at the bus stop for fifteen minutes, becoming absolutely drenched in the rain, earning the leers and scorn of the passersby, than be one of those kids who shows up to school wearing black Hefty bags with three holes torn for their arms and head. My friends and me make fun of those kids, Grandma. We're poor bur we're not *nerds*. I must retain my soggy pride.

I considered just calling in sick. But no.

Why didn't my family just buy me an umbrella? Why was every little convenience some extravagant conceit that only "those *bolillos*" had?

Or why didn't I just buy an umbrella with my summer job money, instead of spending it all on thrift store clothing, pizza, and records?

Teeth gritted, legs dragging, fists clenched, I walked to the pantry to get a glowing white Glad kitchen bag with festive red drawstring. I would just hold it above my head and walk very quickly, I decided. My grandma watched me and rolled her eyes.

Why haven't I bought myself an umbrella by now? What's my excuse? I have a nice car/job/apartment and enough money in the bank to get a big striped umbrella with a wooden duck head for the handle. Not to brag, but I have enough money to get two.

I listened to the hard wet drumming and knew that merely holding the bag above my head wouldn't be enough. Sadly, I began to slit the bag down one of its sides, making a 13-gallon plastic tent. By the time I sawed through the resistant drawstring with my keys, I was giggling a tiny bit hysterically, imagining the impression I'd make on any neighbor passing by.

My grandma glares sternly, ghostly arms materializing to cross at her chest, as I carefully drape the pointed little tarp over my head and shoulders. It floats weightless around me, my pretty sweater, my silver earrings, my make-upped eyes.

I'm not a poor kid. I'm a fine lady in a white *mantilla*. I'm a beautiful industrial bride.

My grandma makes the tsk noise, probably, but I don't hear. I totter quickly through the lot, jump over the long puddle to my silver Nissan carriage. Throw down my costume on the cement before cocooning into my chariot and flying happily away.

I don't know if my grandma's ghost dissipated back into limbo, or if she had to cool her heels in the foyer until the rain died down. I don't know why she doesn't float over to the mall or the movies instead of coming over to criticize me all the time.

When it rains, I always tearfully vow to buy myself an umbrella. When the sun comes out again, I think of the future instead.

Love and Animals

Carnival Macho

She wants to go to the carnival so you take her. You don't wanna spend the gas to drive all across town but then you see her and she's looking nice, so you say it's all right. Borrow money from your dad. You'll work extra next weekend.

Pay for the parking, park in the mud, have to wash the truck tomorrow. She's all happy so it's all right. Need a new muffler. Maybe you'll get some tonight, make this shit's all worth it.

Pay for the tickets. Ride the rides. Tacos. Drinks. Cotton candy.

Stand in line for some big scary-ass roller coaster. She's scared but she's all giggling. You're gonna hold her. It's gonna be all right.

Some fucker bumps into you and cuts in line. Big-ass redneck with all his friends. Fuck him. Keep cool. It's all right.

Motherfucker's looking, laughing at you with all his friends. Now they're looking at her. Checking her out. Looking all over her. She looks down. What's she gonna do? Nothing? She looks back up. She says, "What the . . . " You tell her to be quiet. You say, "It's all right."

Fuck those sons of bitches making all their noise. She says, "C'mon, let's go, I don't want to ride that thing, anyway."

You say, "Fine."

Y'all walk away. You say, " . . . if you're scared."

Punk-ass says, "Wetback." She acts like she didn't hear but you're not fucking stupid.

Y'all keep on walking but she doesn't say nothing.

She says she's tired. You say you wanna ride the rides. Get a goddamned candy apple. You're not gonna leave 'til you're ready.

Some fucker says, "Hey, man, get your girl a Tweety Bird." Basketballs going in the hoop.

Yeah, she's your girl; you'll get her the goddamned Tweety Bird. When he does it, the shit goes in the hoop. When you do it, the shit bounces off the wall.

Fucked up shit. You do it again.

"C'mon, man. Three more dollars for your girl."

Stupid fucking shit. You do it again.

"C'mon, big man. If my girl was that pretty, I'd get her a prize."

This shit's fucking rigged. Do it again.

She says, "C'mon, baby, I'm tired. I don't want a prize. Let's go home."

You say, "Shut the fuck up. Just shut up and let me win."

To the Last Man I Slept with and All the Jerks Just Like Him

After years of trying to fight it, I've decided that I want to look cheap. Blonde highlights, big earrings, red lipstick, too-tight skirts with cellulite rolling out underneath—that's what I've had set my heart on and what I've come back to after all these years. There's no use pretending to be any better by buying clothes from stores where the sales clerks shame me, by resisting the urges when glittery, not-gold displays catch my magpie eyes.

I'm a cheap slut, if that means what I think it does. I don't ask for diamonds before I have sex with you for free. You don't have to buy the cow—you're getting the milk for free. (But I'm not a cow, no matter how much I hear it when I put on that skirt.)

And you ask me why I wanna look like all the other women you've known (even while you wonder what the hell I'm doing with you in the first place). And then you realize anew what you've known all along: all women are whores, and the best you can hope for is to save up enough money to own one who will only be a whore for you. And, actually, you haven't spent any money on me at all, so I must be even worse than the whore that you know all women to be.

So what's left for me to do? I'm damned if I do and lonely if I don't, right? So I'll be damned.

Bring on the cheap stuff. Glitter on my eyes, silver on my toes. Hard nipples through a tight t-shirt. My hair like I just dragged myself out of your bed and walked down the humid street to see who else was out there—not with the blank face of "I can't hear you whistling at my body parts" but with the head-toss and smirk of, "Don't be whistling, buddy, unless you're sure you can last a night with me."

Spend the dollar on gasoline and treat yourself to me. I'm a cheap piece of meat. Heat me up tonight. I'm cheap like sugar and food coloring—I'm the big Barbie birthday cake you buy a little girl when you can't afford to send her to college. Cut me up, eat me up, forget about it. I'm cheap like paper—a golden piñata shining in the sun. Fill my holes with your sweet stuff, hombre. Smack me around a little. Then go on your way. Give another man a chance to use his stick. Pull me down from the sky and tear me apart. Take everything I had inside, then smash it into the ground.

Ants

nts have been on my mind a lot lately. (Not literally, but you know.) We get lots of them in the summer. There are the big red ones outside, and the little black ones inside. The red ones bite me when I'm working in the garden. My anger at them is always tempered with grudging respect. I'll put my foot near the edge of a flowerbed so I can pull out a weed, and the ants will start attacking me. I'll yell, "Dammit! Ow! Die, you little red bastards!" But then I'll realize that these ants are running out and braving the Giant Foot to *save their people*, and I'll have to coo, "Aw!"

The black ants never bite me. They just come in to eat the food that the kids have dropped around the dining table. I used to freak out when I saw them and run to douse them with bleach, brake cleaner, or whatever was on hand. Or else I'd get my oldest shoes—the ones with no treads left—and use them to pound the ants into the floor.

But I don't kill them anymore. Why should I? They're only looking for food. It's hot outside and there's nothing but bugs and abandoned garden tomatoes for them to eat. There must be billions of ants out there, in our town. Or maybe even billions in my back yard alone. It must be like some kind of impossible dream when a colony of ants discovers the way through my kitchen door. I can just see the first ant coming in. He pulls himself up through the crack and, suddenly, the air is cool. It's alien. "Weird," he thinks. Maybe he's a little scared. But he goes on. He is a scout, determined to complete his mission.

When he gets under the table, he stops and stares. (Or waves his little feelers around. Whichever.) It's like mounds of shining treasure in the pyramids of Egypt or something. Tortilla crumbs! Bread crumbs! Little bits of cheese! And— oh, my ant goddess!—a pool of melted Popsicle!

But he doesn't know the brand names, of course. He just smells the food. He senses the sugar. They all like sugar, you know. They're just like me. Well, not like me at all, really. But they do like sugar.

And they work so hard. There's no telling how much organization it takes to get them all into the house and out again with the food in tow. Some people think that colonized insects must be telepathic. Either way, their systematic workflow is impressive.

Ants really like to congregate in the piles of dirty laundry, I've found. And I can't help but notice that they like to hang out in the crotches of my panties. Sometimes they eat holes into the fabric.

This might be sick, but I find that sort of flattering.

Not so flattering that I'd make up long involved fantasies about it, of course. I mean, I would never sit around and imagine large ants from outer space kidnapping me so that they could tie me up and then stimulate the pleasure center in my brain with real-seeming holographic scenarios about attractive celebrities being romantically interested in me, all so that the giant space ants could harvest the precious crotches from my panties and the nourishing juices contained therein.

Or that a cornerstone of their alien economy rests on the sale of said juices and therefore makes my pleasuring an absolutely vital cause, requiring a huge lab and Research and Development Department to sustain it.

No, I would never think about it to that extent, because that would be wrong. I'm just saying that it's interesting that ants like laundry. Isn't it?

When I see them on my sink now, I apologize quietly and then try to kill them quickly. I smash them with the tip of my finger, hoping it was fast enough to be painless. When I see them on the floor, I use my broom. While I'm sweeping them out the back door, I wonder how they're rationalizing it all in their little ant minds. Do they survive the fall? Are they afraid as they rush through the air? When they get to the ground, how do they figure out where they are? Are there other ants around to tell them? Maybe they fall, and the other ants rush up and exclaim, "Dude, I saw you! You FLEW out of that house!" Or do they become completely disoriented and wander around for days until they die? What if they meet another ant tribe before they can make it home? Are they given a membership application, or does the local ant police pick them up and haul them away? Who knows? Does anyone care besides me?

If I could speak Ant language and interview one of these brave scouts, what would I say?

"Just tell me, sir—*were my panties worth it?*"

Ha. Just kidding. I would never think about such a thing. But, if I did, I can't help but imagine that the answer would always be yes.

In Heat

*H*e is behind the house. He is big and white and I want him bad. I walk by, pretending not to see. He wants me bad, too, now.

He fights with the others. He hurts them and they run away. I roll on the concrete in my lust. He comes to me, bleeding, ready. "Get away!" I say. "You disgust me!" He takes me, anyway. It is so good, I scream.

The same thing happens again. They are all good. White, black, and orange. I am tired and I tell them to go away. I mean it this time, so they go.

I am so, so hungry. And I itch. I call to the woman so that she will feed me. I touch her. Sometimes she scratches me, but sometimes she's lazy. I touch her because sometimes she scratches me.

I had a hard night, and now I have children.

My children are hungry. I will feed them. They are dirty, too. I will lick them. I play with them and hold them while we sleep.

I love my children, but they get on my nerves. They need to find their own food.

My children keep eating my food. They need to learn how to call the woman and make her feed them, too. I'm hungry. I love my children but they're pissing me off. Who is that? Is that someone who used to be my child? Get out of here! Get your own food! Go find your own house!

Finally, I'm getting some rest and there is enough food for everyone.

I see a gray cat. I want him bad.

To the Last Man I Slept with and All the Jerks Just Like Him (Revised)

*W*hen is it going to be enough for you?

Anything you wanted, I gave you. You wanted me to be yours alone. I was. You wanted me to live with you. I did. You wanted me to take care of you, the frightened child. I cared. You wanted me to give you space. I gave it.

You wanted to be the smart one. I shut my mouth. You wanted to be the funny one. I shut my mouth. You wanted me to prove my love. My friends wonder why they never hear from me anymore.

I do love you. I do want us to be happy. That's why, every time you say that things could be perfect—that you could love me better if I would just change myself or rearrange my life—I do. All I want is for us to be happy together. Baby, I'm tired of fighting, too.

I do whatever you want. Isn't that enough?

I let you do whatever you want. Isn't that enough?

I won't do anything unless you want. Isn't that . . .

I'll be quiet and wait for you to tell me what you want. Is that . . .

Just correct me when I'm wrong. Just show me when I'm wrong. You just make me see I'm wrong. You make me understand. I know I'm too stupid to do it on my own. Tell me louder if you have to. Scream it in my ear. Throw the bottle against the wall if it helps you make your point.

Shake some sense into me. I know you don't want to hurt me, you just want me to understand what it is that you . . . Shake me. Hit me. I run. Call me back and explain it all again. I think I almost understand . . . Don't you see, baby? I think I finally understand what you want. No . . . hit me again. I stay, waiting. Drag me by my hair. Hit me until I understand. Tell me why I'm always wrong, why I'll always be too stupid to understand, why I'm too worthless for anyone else to try to take the time to make me understand, why I'm lucky you're the only one who cares enough to try to make us happy, why you hit me, slap me, kick me, beat me, bite me, burn me, scream at me, laugh at me, ignore me, humiliate me, love me the way I obviously don't deserve.

I forgot—what was the question again?

The Bus Driver

*E*very afternoon you fall for his sad black hair and haunted eyes.

This isn't a pale, corporate, middle-class, white dough-man like you can see every day at your desk high in the sky. This is a man who will sweat. The only kind you've ever known. You look at him and he looks back. His eyes make you ache.

He's a bus driver.

❧

Your best friend says, "He's a bus driver. God, please don't tell me you're gonna get all crazy over a bus driver. Why can't you pick somebody decent for once? Or, better yet, why can't you just be by yourself for a while? Just sit back and wait. You only find love when you're least suspecting it. Don't be desperate. Desperation shows. Just be happy and self-confident and the right man will come along."

She doesn't really say all that, but you can tell by her face that she's thinking it. Again.

"I gotta go. Me and Julio have to look at halls for our reception."

Maybe he's not just a bus driver. Maybe he's secretly an artist. And you're not desperate, either. You're just…

෨ංණ

Your mother says, "He probably has a pregnant girl-friend at home. He probably deals drugs. He probably picks up old ladies at bars, gives them the best sex of their lives, then steals their purses. You always pick men like that—men like your goddamned father."

(No, she didn't say that. Your mother's dead, remember?)

He doesn't *have* to do those things. Or, if he does do those things, it's probably only because no one ever loved him. If you had the chance, you'd . . .

෨ංණ

Your father says, "He probably just wants to use you for your money. Don't let him, honey. Hey, do you mind running down to the store? We ran out of beer."

He's drunk. What does he know?

Maybe you don't mind buying a few lunches, a few dinners, even a few shirts or gallons of gasoline, to be with a man this handsome who's starving for your love. Money is something you can spare on love. Maybe he's secretly a musician and you can snuggle on the couch as you watch your favorite movies and he can write songs for you and you can help him get a better job . . .

෨ංණ

The face on the magazine says, "Yeah, sure he likes you. If he has a fetish for fat asses. Not to mention your acne and chin hair. Why don't you whiten your teeth before you get carried away imagining that a man would find you attractive?"

It's airbrushed. Don't listen.

Maybe he doesn't mind your fat. Or maybe he actually

likes the way you look. Maybe he sees your inner beauty. Maybe he sees that you're secretly an artist . . .

∂∼⌐

The devil says, "He's watching you. He thinks about you every night. He wants to squeeze your fat ass in his hands and laugh in your face while you come. And it's gonna be the best fucking sex of your life. Go get him. All it takes is a six pack. A bottle of tequila. A bag of weed. Just show him the money. Hell, show him your panties. He'll know what to do. Sure, he'll treat you bad, but you can treat him bad, too. When's the last time you felt good mixed with bad, instead of just bad? Do it. Do it now. Do it all night. Call in sick tomorrow. Quit your job. Drive to Mexico. Fuck everybody. Drink. Come. Laugh. Don't comb your hair. Kill somebody. Who cares what you do? Nobody cares about you. Do whatever you want."

No . . . no . . . There's a rosary at home, in your dresser drawer. Don't listen to the devil.

You twist and sweat, alone in your bed. Maybe . . . maybe . . . maybe . . .

∂∼⌐

Your high heels click down the street. Don't listen, don't listen, their rhythm says. Don't think, don't think, they say when you walk faster.

The bus door opens. Don't look, don't look.

The bus driver says, "Hi."

What do you say?

You say, "Hi. I love you. I know you don't love me yet, but please say you'll come with me and let me love you. I know no one else sees the good in you, but I see it, and I know that you'll be able to see the good in me. I've been dreaming about you for weeks. I've been carrying around this love, these dreams, this sickly sweet baby-talking affection in my chest. Nobody's ever appreciated it before and it wells up inside me, just waiting for the right man. Let me love you. I know I can make us happy. I'll do everything. All I need is for you to look at me and say that you believe it. I love you. Let me make you happy."

The bus driver looks straight ahead. He pulls the crank that closes the door and drives his bus down the street. He's not looking at you anymore.

He doesn't hear you.

But I hear you. And I know exactly what you mean.

To the Last Man I Slept with and All the Jerks Just Like Him (For Real this Time)

I thought you were supposed to be the brave one.

I thought you were the brave one, motherfucker. You keep on telling me how you fought in the war, how you fight in the bars, how you fight in your mind every Saturday night after you've had your beer. You make the big bucks. You swing the tools. You've got the upper body strength. You're not a pussy, because pussies are weak, right?

Am I supposed to admire you because you hit people to make a point? Am I supposed to be afraid of you because you hurt people, because you're afraid that if you don't, one of your kind will call you a faggot or, worse, a *woman*?

I'm braver than you will ever be. The difference between you and me is that I have the guts to say that I'm afraid. I'm not so scared of what others think that I have to hide it when I get hurt. I don't have to get drunk to have an excuse to cry. When I hurt, I cry out loud. I call all my friends on the phone and say, "Ow. I am hurting." I rip off my bodice and go bleed in the middle of the street so everyone can see my wounds while I go to pick up my laundry. I BUY MY SANITARY NAPKINS AT THE DRUG STORE AND I DON'T CARE WHO KNOWS IT.

I hurt, I cry, I bleed, and then I pick myself up and move on. I don't take it out on someone smaller than me. I don't numb myself with chemicals and then cry and hug my buddies and then form a gang with them so we can beat up another gang of crying drunk guys at a bar. I don't make up elaborate games so I can hug my buddies and touch their asses and then throw a football and go break the bones of a team of other guys who hug each other and touch each others' asses.

I tell my friend, "You look pretty." If we feel like it, we cry. I don't call my buddies and say, "Hey, let's form a special club for men only where we can wear special uniforms or make secret rules and then gang-rape women and beat the shit out of faggots and then lie for each other so it'll last forever." I know you do all that just so you can get drunk enough to play one of those games involving our penises (that aren't homo because you say so.) Then, late at night, right before you slip into a drunken stupor with blood on your fists, you can finally look down at my buddy and think, just for a split second, "You are pretty." Or whatever it is that you guys do. I don't understand it. All I know is that it isn't brave.

ॐ

My *pussy* is braver than you. I let you fuck me and then my pussy will push out one of your kind (and, yeah, it hurts—you know it does) and, as long as you stay out of my way, I'll make him a better man than you even know how to be.

You wanna know the bravest thing about me? It's that even though I *know* how you are—how all your type is—how you, in the name of bravery, will hit me, rape me, degrade me, clitorectomize me, and make sure I get paid less than you. . . . Even though I know all that, I'm *still* brave enough to go outside. I'm so brave, I go out every day and talk to you, listen to you, buy from you, date you, work with you, dance with you, marry you, care for you, defend you, and put up with your bullshit.

Not anymore, though. Hell no. This is the end of the line. I'm not putting up with your weakness anymore. I don't need you. I never respected you. I've learned my lesson and now I hate you.

You're a coward.

Get away from me.

Aunt Rosie

For years I believed what they said about Aunt Rosie and repeated it mindlessly to myself and others, like something you mutter in church. "He treats her that way because she lets him. I wouldn't let no man do that to me." I laughed at my uncle's jokes and let him kiss me on the cheek. I shook my head along with the others when he yelled at Aunt Rosie and she scurried to bring him another beer.

He continued to yell at her and call her names while I grew up, moved away, and got a man of my own. My uncle yelled and forced my aunt to scurry at his will until, full of tumors and Budweiser, he exploded. She cried hardest at the funeral. Her strength, it seemed, had lain in holding out until he died.

If I had problems of my own, my strength would have been secrecy. No matter what happened, no one would ever say that I let it happen. No one would say that I deserved what I got. If I had problems, I would be strong, taking it like a man—or, like a woman, actually—keeping up the front with no whining. I would have taken it until I was filled with anger, fear, and poor self-esteem, and then—right before I exploded—I would have escaped and gone back home.

When I got back home, I saw that Aunt Rosie had changed. Now she laughed. She wore small tiny clothes in blazing colors, drove fast in a pick-up, and danced all night long. She had fun times with men. Very fun times with lots of men.

I only saw her for bright flashes at a time. The phone would ring and, if she weren't pressed for time, she'd pick it up and murmur the quick, sweet lies I've heard murmured to me so many times. "Yeah, baby. You know I do. Yeah, I'll be there. Uh huh, me too."

The rest of our family told me that she had fun with men every single weekend and sometimes even in public, too. I smiled. They told me again, explaining it more slowly this time so that I would know to snicker, instead, or to roll my eyes. But then I only sighed.

I don't point out to my family members that they're full of shit because the last time I did, everyone uncomfortably joked that my uncle was there, floating around that house, listening. His own daughters said so. They said they heard his angry rumblings at night. But I wasn't scared that he would fly up and slap my face. I figured the very most he could do was knock over a cheap vase whenever he got a well-deserved eyeful of Aunt Rosie exercising her basic rights as an human being in America.

"I don't care if you hear me, Uncle Joe! You know you treated her wrong!" I called floor-ward. Everyone quivered. But Uncle Joe couldn't deny my words, so he didn't say anything at all.

However, since that day, I no longer push the subject. If I did, I'd have to back up my arguments with examples from my own life. And that always leads to them telling me, "If you were having problems, you should have told us. We would have . . ."

They would have helped me, they claim. They would have stopped it. They would have kicked my husband's ass.

They say that stuff and then I very clearly imagine/remember them (her own daughters included) saying, "He treats her that way because she lets him"—this time meaning me.

So I let them change the subject. I watch Aunt Rosie run

out the door in a furious rush to fit in one more good time, before it's too late. I don't tell her what I really want to say, maybe because I don't want to remind her of the times that I did the same shit everybody else did. I guess I'm ashamed of the way I used to be.

I turn to my own children. "Don't listen to ghosts," I say. "And go give your Aunt Rosie a kiss before she goes. Tell her to have a good time."

To the Last Man I Slept with, and to Everybody Else

I spent a lot of time trying to make you the hero. I helped you hold up your front by smiling and nodding at your stories and excuses. I saved you again and again from feeling less than a man, from loneliness and despair, and from the opinions of my friends.

I just realized who the real hero is here.

You wanted to be the rock star, the ninja, the cowboy in black. I wanted to be with those people so I pretended they were you. But secretly, I have always been *all* of those things. I kept it a secret for *you*.

I'm the rock star. I'm the brave warrior. I'm the clever girl who grows up to win fame and fortune. I am the queen. And I always have been.

For years, I could have shown myself as the hero and gotten the credit I deserved. Instead, I've been wasting my time and energy on trying to save you. And now I don't have a damned thing to show for it.

And now I don't have any more time to lose.

༄

I'm going to go out into the world and be a hero. If you want to, you can watch.

Low Brow

My Lord Alpha Male

Chapter 1

Miss Chastity Fairbody looked around in dismay as she alit from the post chaise. Surely this was a very odd part of town in which to find a modiste.

Dusting off her pelisse, Chastity's firm little chin jutted out in a gesture of determination that those who knew her would have recognized all too well. Rough part of London or not, she would be a silly peagoose to back away now and give up the job of assistant modiste, losing the only chance to make a respectable living that had materialized since her father had finally drunk himself to death after gambling away the family estate just six short months ago.

Stubborn wisps of dark, golden, auburn hair escaped from her bonnet, curling into tendrils around her enormous violet eyes. There was no doubt that Chastity was a beauty, had she but known it. Not even the hours spent in front of her mirror, staring at her own reflection while a maid labored over her hair and continually murmured compliments, had managed to affect her modest opinion of herself.

Finally plucking up enough courage to actually move, Chastity stepped towards a small man covered in soot and said in her low, musical voice, "Excuse me, but I wonder if you could tell me . . ."

The chimney sweep was precluded from answering by the sudden interruption of a formidable shadow falling across his face. Chastity glanced toward the source of this awe-inspiring shade, and immediately regretted doing so, as her heart leapt into her throat and then fell all the way down to her tiny slippers.

Standing before her was a—a *man* . . . Oh, but what a specimen of man he was! From the top of his midnight black hair to the soles of his gleaming Hessians, he radiated the very air of elegance. His powerful shoulders strained the blue superfine of an exquisitely tailored coat. His buff-colored breeches clung to his muscular legs so closely . . . each manly bulge outlined by the thin cloth . . .

Chastity blushed at her sudden willingness to consider parts of the male wardrobe she had never, ever considered before, not even after spending hours watching the bulls and stallions on her uncle's farm. Then, looking up and seeing the gentleman's eye monstrously distorted in his quizzing glass, she blushed even redder as she realized he must know the object of her unsettling thoughts.

She needn't have worried. Lord Hawksington, Fifth Earl of Northingham, Viscount Crumswell, Baron of Lint, known by friends and enemies alike as "Mr. Naughty" (being that "The Devil's Cub," "The Rake," "Lord Scandalous," and "Beelzebub's Buddy" were already in use that Season) was not looking at her face.

Never had Hawksington seen such a dashing figure on a female. His eyes bore straight through the faded gray silk of her gown and beheld her slender girl-like form, which was pleasingly thin, like a willow tree in winter, yet also possessed of lush womanly curves. Taking this in quickly, Hawksington next noticed that, although her dress was dowdy, it was still that of a lady. He raised his quizzing glass and looked into the girl's eyes, now shining blue from her flustered state.

"I am Hawksington at your service. Are you in need of assistance?" he asked, giving a slight bow with his head.

Chastity dropped a quick curtsy, nearly tripping over her own dainty feet as she stared into the cool, silver eyes regarding her from beneath dark and forbidding quizzically raised brows and above an indeed hawk-like aristocratic nose and a malevolently, disdainfully, sinfully, knowingly sensuous mouth.

"I—uh—My lord uh—am—um . . ."

Her eyes turned hazel from her efforts to speak sensibly while he watched her like a hawk watches its petite prey

"I am looking for Madame DuPont's." There! Now, hopefully, he would tell her where to find Madame's boutique and she could be left to her own thoughts—fantasies of marrying him and not having to work as a seamstress.

Madame DuPont's! Lord Hawksleigh raised his brow so high that his carefully arranged coif almost revealed his receding hairline. This young girl had managed to throw him off the scent. She was no Lady of Quality, but merely a country wench on her way to work in a brothel! Quickly his manner changed.

"Well, my dear, it just so happens I was headed that way myself. Would you grant me the honor of letting me be your escort?"

Chastity breathed a sigh of relief.

"Yes, my lord. I should like it above all things."

She placed her hand demurely on his arm, only to find herself pulled disarmingly close. She flushed warmly as he led her down the street, altogether too entranced to make conversation. Before she knew it, he had stopped in front of a shady-looking townhouse. Chastity looked at him askance.

"My lord?"

Turning her around to face him, he took her tiny hand

into his own large one, and with his other hand, tipped up her chin.

"Here is the house of Madame DuPont. But before you enter, my dear, will you not tell me your name?"

Dizzily gazing into his eyes, she said breathlessly, "Chastity . . . Miss Chastity Fairbody, my lord."

"What a lovely name for such a lovely creature. Perhaps I will call on you later this evening, once you are situated. I'd like to be the first man in London to sample your wares."

With an arrogant sneer that took away what little breath she had left in her sparse body, Lord Hawksinger leaned down and kissed her, plundering the soft ripe sweetness of her mouth with his tongue. Chastity had never been kissed before. She felt that she was falling into a long, dark abyss of torpid desires never before experienced and only partially recognized by something primal, deep within her very soul. Her senses whirled and her hands grasped at the stranger's shoulders of their own volition, desperate to hang on to something lest she be lost forever in the sweet, fiery passion engulfing them both.

Lord Hawkerton had kissed many women in his three-and-thirty years, but never had he experienced such strange, maddening sweetness as this. Something about this young country lass—something about her delicate frailty, the warmth of her skin, the smallness of her feet, and her obvious inexperience—made him really horny. But underlying that horniness was a need to protect her, the same way he'd like to protect a baby bird whose mother he'd just blown away on the hunting fields. It was an unnerving sensation, and before it got the better of him, he broke away from her lips.

Rudely disjointed from his arms and the world of pleasure they contained, Chastity snapped into awareness of the present and, her eyes blazing with a fury magnificent to behold, hauled off and slapped Lord Hawkerty's face. "Sirrah, you go too far!"

Rubbing his jaw, he admired the fire in her eyes. What a little hellcat she was!

"I pray you will forgive me, my sweet. It didn't occur to me that you might prefer payment beforehand." And with his maddeningly suave smile, he withdrew a sovereign and pressed it caressingly into her palm.

"Grrlph!" shrieked Chastity in her rage. "You, sir, are no gentleman!"

With that harsh set-down, she turned and marched proudly away, her back ramrod straight and her head held high. It wasn't until a few moments later that she remembered the gold piece in her hand, but by then it really was too late to turn and fling it at him without spoiling the whole effect, so she decided instead to use it to hire a hack to take her to the house of the rich, fashionable Great-Aunt Theodora she'd just remembered who lived in Grosvenor Square. Chastity decided she'd throw herself on the grand lady's mercy and just keep this embarrassing little incident to herself.

Her hand flew to her lips as she wondered how she could ever forget.

Lord Hawk watched her go, wondering what he had done to give her such a disgust of him. What a queer little minx. Quite a stunner, though. Not that it mattered, because he'd probably never see her again. He sighed and suddenly, inexplicably, felt quite sad.

Glancing at his watch, he realized it was time to go back to his flat and change. He'd have to hurry if he intended to escort his mother to Lady Theodora's tea on time.

Chapter 2

Lady Theodora was bored. The last thirty years of her life had been an endless round of balls, routs, and croquet games. She was old and overweight.

Just then, the butler announced Miss Chastity Fairbody.

"Great-Aunt Theodora!"

"Chastity! My favorite great-niece!"

The older woman, who was the daughter of an earl and therefore very rich, took one look at the delicate young beauty and noticed that Chastity's dusty black pelisse was torn at the hem immediately. Lady Theodora remembered that she had read in the paper that Chastity's father had died.

Chastity looked at her great aunt and saw that not only was she very rich, she was old and fat. She wore a purple turban with a ruby and yellow ostrich feathers, because she was fat and comical, but also because she had a heart of gold.

"Oh, my dear! We must get you into some more appropriate garments! It's almost time for the dowager and her son to join us for tea! And from now on, until you snag yourself a husband, you will live here with me and I will buy you an elegant wardrobe."

Hastily dropping a curtsy and demurely murmuring her thanks, Chastity was commandeered by a maid who led her to her room. The abigail presented her with a round morning gown of sprigged muslin, which would have been beautiful had it not been so huge, being that it was one of Lady Theodora's. But the maid came with her sewing box and, after a nip here and a tuck there, the dress fit Chastity's lushly petite figure to perfection.

As she walked back down the stairs, it occurred to Chastity that she hadn't yet eaten that day. She felt that she could drink a whole half cup of tea and perhaps even nibble the edge of a biscuit. She hoped to be able to restrain herself and behave with ladylike decorum so as not to embarrass her great-aunt in front of her guests. Just then, Chastity heard voices coming from the Burnt Orange Salon, where she had left Lady Theodora. The guests had arrived! Chastity quickened her step down the remaining few stairs.

She was the very picture of maidenly, yet sexy, womanhood as she stood in the doorway of the Burnt Orange Salon. However, she had no inkling of the fact because first of all, she was very modest, and second of all, her attention was immediately caught and held, like a sweet little mouse in a falcon's sharp grasp, by one in particular of her great aunt's guests.

"Ah, my dear Miss Fairbody. We were beginning to despair of your ever—ahem—coming."

It couldn't be! It was! It was that heinous rogue, Lord Hawksleigh!

Chastity's eyelashes fluttered as her eyes rolled up in her head and she daintily slid to the floor in a faint.

Chapter 3

Chastity awoke with her cheek nestling against something hard as stone yet soft as velvet. Her long dark lashes fluttered upwards and saw with a gasp that it was Lord Hawkley's bicep! She immediately fainted again.

The second time she came to, it was to a strange sense of freedom and relaxation.

"Gracious, child, but you did have your corset on too tight!" started Lady Theodora. Chastity didn't hear as she was staring into dark, hawk-like, ebony eyes that seemed to see right through her corset, stays, and bodice.

"If Miss Fairbody is not feeling quite the thing, perhaps it would be better if Mother and I took our leave now," his full, moist, masculine lips seemed to say. Chastity shook her delicate head, came out of her daze, and for the first time noticed the Duke's mother, the Dowager Duchess of Hawksington. She was one of those thin old women with grim faces, so Chastity looked back at Lord Hawk. Her heart beat quickly, like that of a small dainty bird or a gerbil.

"N-n-n-no," she managed to stammer petitely. "D-d-don't go on my account. I'm all right now. I'll just have some tea."

She made her way to the table where Lady Theodora was cheerfully eating a plate of Little-Debbie-like cakelets. But then, Chastity suddenly felt a searing heat come upon her and settle into a tumultuous vortex somewhere in the vicinity of her virgin womb. Realizing it was from Lord Hawksley's eyes, she suddenly lost her appetite.

Lady Theodora winked at the dowager duchess and said, "Mayhap some fresh air would do you good, Chastity. That is, if young Lord Hawk here would be so gracious as to offer you a ride in his curricle." Chastity started in alarm. What could her great-aunt be thinking? Unless it was a plan to get Chastity and Lord Hawk out of the house so Lady Theodora could have more cakes and biscuits for herself . . .

What was it about this man that tied her stomach in knots and made her mouth so dry that she had to lick her lips with her delicate pink tongue whenever he looked her way? Why, he was odious and a rascal and he took liberties with the persons of proper young misses! He disgusted her! That was it, wasn't it?

Or was it that the sight of him in his velvets and laces, combined with his heady smell of leather, snuff, pomade, and rugged un-washed skin, that made her want to tear off her clothes and roll with him in the mud behind the stables, taking whatever it was he had to give her over and over again until he caused her to cry out, "Oh, my Lord!"

No, of course not. That wasn't it at all. Perish the thought. Chastity blushed as she took Lord Hawk's arm and allowed him lead her out the door.

Chapter 4

As her delicate bottom roughly bounced against the creamy leather of the curricle seat, Chastity found herself reaching for his lordship's arm with which to steady herself.

He flashed a malevolent yet boyish grin at her that made her realize that he must have been driving over the pock-marked and manure-strewn roads for just that purpose. *The devil!* she thought to herself. *The handsome, demonic devil!*

As they made their way to the famous Row, all the various nobles stared at them. They did make a handsome couple. Had Chastity but glanced around, she could have seen that she was the only woman over fifteen with a full set of natural teeth. But she had eyes only for the space two inches from Lord Hawk's face. She was too shy, and maybe a little afraid, even, to look right *at* his face. The satanically handsome devil!

"My dear, you seem preoccupied," her companion offered in a voice that was sumptuous and sensual yet facetious and nonchalant.

"Perhaps it is because I'm not used to being so quickly swept away by a personage who, only that morning, had mistaken a lady for a *high flyer*," she retorted pointedly, with a saucy toss of her curls.

"But, my dear, we all make mistakes. Especially when the personage in question has no memory of any other lady so delectably *high-flyable*," he rejoined, his eyebrow teasingly raised.

"That may be, but that doesn't excuse the fact that a *real gentleman* would have offered an immediate apology," flared Chastity, her nostrils flaring as well in fiery challenge.

"Can it be that the lady of which we are speaking has charms which would cause any gentleman to forget all about being gentlemanly?" Lord Hook fired back, his ears wiggling defiantly.

"Could it be that no gentleman would speak to a lady in such a way as you are speaking to me now? Sirrah, I demand recompense!" Her forehead creasing and her lymph nodes pulsing in a way that brooked no defeat, she glared at him as she spoke this last.

"Then you shall have it."

Before Chastity could gather her wits and utilize any more facial tics, she realized that their curricle was parked on a deserted street, away from the crowds. That was all she saw before her lips were descended upon by the brutal force that was Lord Hawk's kiss. His lips only touched hers gently, but they crushed her will to his with the strength of a thousand draft animals.

What new rudeness was this? Oh, and what new unforeseen pleasure? Really, this was nothing like the kisses she had practiced on the scarecrows at home. True, there was the same vague itchiness and smell, but something different, as well. Something wonderfully different. Without even slipping her his tongue, Lord Hawk had managed to send her spinning on a brightly-colored carousel of pleasure around which there was no gate or exit sign, on which there were none of those ugly horses with the chipped paint . . . but all too soon, it was over.

"Oh, my, how divine . . ."

Lord Hawk smiled.

"That is, how divinely rude!" With that, she slapped him roundly on the cheek.

Then, *what have I done?* she wondered. She, an unchaperoned young miss, had just struck this large, strong man in his own curricle, on a deserted road. There was no telling how he might retaliate—in what sordid ways he might seek his revenge. Just for good measure, she slapped him again.

"I beg your pardon, madam. I don't know what came over me. I will, of course, escort you to your aunt's now." And so saying, Lord Hawk signaled his stallions into a U-turn and slowly drove them back into the fashionable crowd.

"Thank you, my lord," Chastity whispered. And then she sighed with relief. Or was it? Was it relief, after all?

Chapter 12

As the storm-tossed sea tossed in its own tormentuous wake, Chastity's heart mimicked it with great skill. *Oh, where is he?* she fretted to herself, in her mind. *Where could that rascal Lord Hawk be?* And had he won her father's fortune back? Or was he being brutally murdered by the villains in the captain's quarters even now?

Her nightgown dewy and semi-sheer with the evidence of her emotional tumult, Chastity's hand strayed below the rough linen of the cabin bunk and up under her negligee to find her comfort. Ah, yes. That was it. That was the spot. Her finger caressed the bright, hard nub of her jewel as she sighed with relief. Yes . . . Lord Hawk's grandmother's famed ruby pendant was still lodged in the top of her woolen stocking.

Just then, his lordship burst into the room.

"Chastity!" he cried. "What are you doing here? I thought I'd seen you safely away on the rowboat!"

"Oh, my lord, please don't be angry with me!" she cried in return, her voice like that of a beautiful young cockatoo. "I simply couldn't leave you here all alone to face your stepbrother, the wicked Duke of Lancome, and all his henchmen! Why, if anything had happened to you . . . I . . . I . . ."

❧❦

"Oh, my silly Chastity. My silly, ridiculous, stupid, darling girl!" Lord Hawk rushed over to her on the bunk and crushed her in his darkly masculine embrace. Before she could protest, his lips found hers and urgently, hungrily, wetly met hers in a kiss that burned like the sinful, sulfurous depths of Hades itself. All gone were the words, the questions that had started to pour forth from her milky rosebud lips. All gone were the thoughts that had, moments ago, filled her tiny glistening head. Oh, to be kissed by such a man on the high seas in a ship full of swarthy, hairy pirates! She was suffused and overwhelmed with the heady wine that was the experience. Again and again he thrust his strong tongue within her gentle mouth as his hard chest pressed against her soft one, the peaks of which were beaten into stiffness by his touch. His hair, his jacket, his watch fob filled her hands as she grasped, grasped . . . grasped at him sightless like a blind beggar after a dropped coin.

"Oh, my darling . . ." she moaned.

"Yes, my sweet creature," he murmured against her ear, sending shock waves exploding like a thunderdome through her spine.

"My darling Lord Hawk . . . Did you win the money back?" she managed to gasp.

He pulled away.

"Actually . . ." he began, "Actually, well, no, I didn't."

There was a moment of silence, and then he began again. "My dyslexia, you know . . . Awfully blasted difficult to call the cards, don't you know . . ."

"Oh, Lord Hawk!" Chastity crestfallenly cried. Whatever will we do now? Without my father's money, here under the duke's power . . . What will become of us?"

Slowly, meticulously, the smile which Chastity had come to know all too well spread itself across Lord Hawk's mouth. When it had finished spreading and his incisors twinkled like lamps freshly lit by a servant, he looked down at her and said, "My darling Chastity, there's no need to worry about that now. For I have a much better idea."

So saying, his hand roughly drew back the scratchy coverlet, exposing Chastity's creamy pearl thighs to his gaze.

"My lord!" Chastity gaspingly cried, her cheeks and eyes ablaze with new flames. "How dare you . . . and she fumbled for the words of indignance, regretting her wanton behavior of a moment ago and the shameful degradation to which it would now undoubtedly—surely, how could it not?—lead. She moistened her lips and arched her back in a delicate show of maidenly modesty.

"Ah, yes," whispered his lordship, slowly lifting the hem of her gown. "This is what I wanted. . . . "

And as Chastity's eyes closed and rolled up in her head in a near-swoon, Lord Hawk plucked the ruby from her garter and sprung from the bed.

"Come, Chastity! We have no time to lose!"

Middle of Chapter 18

, with a kiss that fell on her drenched mouth like a rain of fire.

She ran her hands across his cravat and made noises like a wounded kitten. His gigantic hands stroked her firmly, surely, up and down the bodice of her gown in the back and on the sides. And then his fingers brushed almost within an inch below the most womanly part of the bodice, and she felt herself flush and blush hot and cold with electricity which hadn't yet been discovered unless you counted its sudden appearance on Chastity's flesh.

"Oh, my lord," she sighed, losing her senses to what was right or proper anymore as his hot breath bathed her neck.

"Chastity," he groaned, as an emotion like an arrow with a thick volcanic shaft pierced the very center of his manly feeling.

Suddenly, he pushed her down onto the emerald grass, his muscular form soon closely joining hers as he covered her with his virile hardness and scent.

"What is it, my darling?" she whispered, tossing back her hair and panting like a randy jackal.

"Oh, I'll show you what it is," he husked in his warm, moist baritone. Reaching over her supple form, saying, "I'll show you what it is, all right . . ."

Lord Hawk pointed at the horizon.

"Highwaymen, coming this way. Stay down! I'll be right back!"

Somewhere in Chapter 23

ripped off her bodice, crying, "Oh, my darling, here it is!"

And she quickly wrapped the sprigged muslin around his bloody head, wondering if she'd ever see him conscious again, just when she'd started to think that she realized she didn't hate him so much after all.

Somewhere Near the Beginning of Chapter 30

And so he had finally explained it all, and she couldn't be mad at him any more. "The fortune was rightfully mine all along, and he was a spy for the King!" she thought again, smiling contentedly.

Middle of Chapter 30

"Come sit on my lap, my lovely bride," he rumbled. Just then, Lady Dogatha trotted in with a whole litter of adorable puppies following behind. Chastity's musical giggle tinkled in harmony with Duke Ian Hawk's low chuckle as they laughed and laughed.

Page 297

Up the stairs, onto her satin-coated bed.

"But wait," she said, suddenly remembering. "Whatever happened to the . . .

Page 300

very, very slowly and softly on her brow. And then he sat up and removed her first slipper, stopping to remark on the daintiness and petite rapturous beauty of each toe.

Page 301, which is the last damned page and had better be good

"My darling, darling, darling Duke of Hawkston," she groaned musically as he caressed her swollen bosom

through the silk-ribbon-embroidered microfiber of her shim-
mery lingerie. Her miniscule hands traveled along his rip-
pling chest while he buried his head into the vastness of her
cleavage, kissing her there with wistfully delicious abandon.
Then, with a swirling phantasm of pleasure, he unbuttoned
the top of the gown and exposed her glorious orbs for all of
himself to see.

"You're so, so beautiful. You're the loveliest thing I've
ever seen," he whispered tenderly, moving his fingers lightly along the sides of her large, free-standing mounds. And
then those same fingers touched the tiny buds of passion,
causing a torrent of molten ecstasy to course through her
blood like a freight train.

"My darling!" she moaned orgiastically. "Have all of
me! Have all of me now!"

Before she could cajole him sweetly further, his mouth
was upon those soft, hardened nodules of pleasure at the tips
of her satiny globes. He sucked at them sensuously, eagerly,
deeply, causing her blood to sing with molten joy. She didn't
think such joy was possible, not until, gently pushing her
down among the silken heaps of pillows, he lightly parted
her velvety thighs and, in a heated frenzy of titanic desire,
inserted the male gloriousness of himself into her very core,
all the way up to the fire-driven hilt.

Her head swam in the depths of a passion so intense, it
was as if a thousand rose petals had floated down onto two
thousand pink candles, igniting into a rich, fiery glow that
infused her very soul with its turbulent, torrential, volcanic
warmth. She felt herself falling over into an immense
canyon of searing desire, only to be buoyed up again by a
flowing current of dense, turgid, pure animal lust. And that
sweet, gentle, soft lust slowly swelled beneath her, around
her, alongside her, above . . . bringing with itself a need for
something greater than herself. That sugary need, that soar-

ing want, that heavenly aching within her most womanly center built and carried her higher. And still it built, and built, and built up some more. And then . . .

With one, final, soft kiss, the Duke of Hawklington, her new husband, rolled off of her and next to her side.

"My sweet darling Chastity," he sighed, "you have just made me the happiest man in the world."

With a brilliant smile, the new Duchess closed her pretty eyes and went to sleep.

Fin.

The gai Jin Perspective

WORKING TITLE UNTIL I GET A JAPANESE OR CHINESE DICTIONARY

The second shot grazed his ear. By the third he was plunging into the icy cold water, moving downstream and out of range. He could hold his breath for seven minutes if necessary. But the bomb in his hand had thirty seconds left. If he emerged now he could throw it into the midst of the guerrillas and kill them all. He could also be shot. Better to wait until he'd reached the shadows under the concrete ledge.

There wasn't much time left to consider the matter. His shoulder was starting to ache from the sword gash. The sharks were probably attracted to the smell. He kicked another one away.

Fifteen more seconds.

Just then he remembered: N always set the bomb timers wrong. Dangerous affliction, dyslexia. That meant . . .

Zero. The ashes rained down.

☙❧

Major Anthony Kendrick— -not his real name, of course; no one knew that—watched the woman from across the room. At first he'd thought her a local peasant but the unconvincing rhythm of her tread as she carried him to her hut made him suspicious. Once in front of the fire she removed her yak hide *njingitsa*, revealing a tight, short dress and five-inch heels, and then he knew. She was probably a member of the American press.

She bandaged his forehead. Her breasts jutted before him like fleshy Z19 missiles—the missiles no one knew about but N, the Prime Minister and, of course, him.

"Water?" she asked.

"What's your name?"

Her mouth was all over his. Her tongue moved in quick short thrusts. So much like the other woman. But that was so long ago. How could this woman know about that? So many years ago, and her breasts like grenades . . .

It almost worked. She had succeeded in distracting him for a moment but once he smelled the cordite and mercuric iodide residue in her hair, he knew.

This was the one he'd been searching for.

❧≈❧

The only question now: what action would be best for the Crown? He could easily reach around to her right ear-lobe and smash with his fingers the *lo-tsin-nguyen* point just under the skin, killing her instantly. He could merely disable her optic nerve and then ransack the room. He could give her a really bad case of diarrhea . . .

No. He knew what he would do. Three years of being Commander Kruskatov's whore made a woman useful for one kind of punishment: *Dosinjai.*

The hand reaching to smash her ear instead gave it a hair-trigger-light touch that caused her to moan with intense pleasure. He followed this with a firm slapping motion on her left buttock that was in counterpoint to the rhythm of his pulse. Her moans became louder.

It was all coming back to him. All those years of train-ing at the hands of Master Qxackwan and his many concubines with breasts shaped like a wide variety of things. His years of studying *Dosinjai*, the ancient art of conquering a woman's body with a man's *bo lo nai*.

A deft touch here, a short caress there, a quick poke . . . he was done. She was finished. She had undergone a physical experience so potent it would leave her unable to respond to any other man. She would forget all about The Cause and wander the streets in delirium.

Once again Her Majesty's kingdom was safe.

For now.

How to Be a Trailer Trash Housewife

The Choice

I picked sky-blue for the color of our doublewide, figuring that if I had to become trailer trash, I might as well do so whole-heartedly. The mortgage companies wouldn't entrust us with even the lowliest of houses. My swollen womb called out for a nest. My prejudices had no say.

A thick buffer of half-dead grass separated us from the rest of the neighborhood, leaving me to spy on them in solitude. I saw that there were two clear paths from which to choose.

On the one hand, bright aluminum foil gleamed from windows below in which objects existed without explanation or shame. Beer cans, broken appliances, dogs, cats, carburetors, Christmas lights, cacti, old calendars, chickens, children, doilies, afghans, colored bottles, Easter baskets, tomato plants, seashells, tankless toilets—all of it splatter-painted across yards, living rooms, kitchen tables in not reckless but perfectly languid abandon.

Wasn't it art?

Where else could an American be that free?

But how did one avoid the salmonella and the fleas?

My alternative, on the other hand, was the battle to legitimize mobile home living—to pretend it was middle class. A tidy beige manufactured home filled with slipcovers and cozies, imitation-wood paneling hiding the fact that it was all on wheels. All of it bought on credit from Wal-Mart or Fingerhut.

Fingerhut catalogues were (as required by law?) mailed to every trailer in the world every month. They showed us beautiful toasters, leather-look jackets, and gun racks available for just ten dollars a month, just ten years, for just ten times the price by the time the interest had all been paid. I heard someone accidentally call it Fingerfuck once, a most appropriate Freudian slip on the sweepstakes contests or the government-sponsored lotteries. They don't just want to screw us out of our money, they want to tenderly, teasingly tickle it out of us, bit by bit, leaving cheap gifts on our plywood dressers in return.

I straddled the fence between the proud-to-be trailer trash and the modular-home gentry trash. It was so hot and dusty outside, so air-conditioned and mind numbing inside. Living in a mobile home made it easy to put off decision-making for a while.

The Mail

Every morning, I went out to get the mail. Sometimes I went two or three times a morning, then once or twice in the afternoon, becoming more frustrated and desperate if it wasn't there. Calling the post office to bawl them out like you would a drunken husband.

After a while I stopped hoping for letters from friends or the notification that I had won a million dollars. But I could always count on the catalogs. Usually there were at least two or three, more on a good day. I would hug them tightly to my breast and run them through the flames shot down by the Hill Country sun, crashing through the front door and then safe to my bed, kids and cats calling far behind.

There was a procedure to follow. No straying or short-

cuts allowed. First, I looked at the entire catalog, one page at a time. My favorites were the ones with clothing in my size—Lane Bryant, Roaman's, Big Beautiful Fashions for Her. But I perused anything the mailbox awarded me: house wares, garden bulbs, cowboy boots, lingerie. After a long, leisurely flip through the glossy images, I had a good sense of what version of happiness they were offering: Affordable style. Timeless classics. Decadent luxury. Plain old sex.

After the last page, I would lovingly set the catalog on my bedside table, gaze at the ceiling for a while, then get up and resume my chores. Clothes always needed washing. Children wanted to be fed.

This gave the catalog time to rest, to regenerate, before I picked it up again. The second reading was a little more intent. Ostensibly, I was just doing the same thing all over again—flipping through the pages. But this time, I was choosing items. If I could pick one item from each page, which would it be?

That was fun. Some day soon I might have money to buy something, and it was good to be ready, wasn't it? To take advantage of an opportunity before it slipped away. Picking only one thing from each page, whether it was something I wanted or not, made it a fun little game. Like the time limit that keeps the game show shopping spree from getting out of control. A necessary balance.

I liked to try to do the whole catalog in one sitting. If someone needed my attention while I was performing this ritual, my one bit of fun and relaxation of the day, I'd sigh, fold down the page's corner to save my place, and hurry through my duties as quickly as I could. I tried to schedule my catalog games during propitious blocks of time, while the baby was nursing or, later, when all the kids were mesmerized by their favorite television programs. Once I got through the whole thing, the catalog was hidden away in a drawer until the third reading.

The third reading was an additional process I developed over time, something *extra* fun reserved for when I was feeling particularly stressed by the demands of motherhood and household management.

The scenario was that the catalog company had awarded me a thousand-dollar shopping spree. Or five thousand dollars, depending on the scale of its merchandise. Or a hundred dollars if the mailbox had been infuriatingly barren that week and I'd had to resort to pulling drugstore sales flyers from the Sunday paper. I had to pick items that totaled as close to that limit as possible, even if it meant pretend-purchasing eighteen butterfly-shaped napkin rings in order to do so. Then I was the winner and all the time I had spent adding up the prices was well spent.

The third reading took longer than the first two, since I had to add the figures in my head and wasn't allowed to use paper or even to write down the subtotal when the baby cried. When the baby cried, I'd just keep that subtotal in my mind until I could resume the game later. I'd chant it in my mind. *Four thirty-seven fifty-three*, over and over again. Sometimes I'd say it aloud when someone asked me a question.

Because of this side effect, I tried to save my third readings for late at night, when everyone else in the house was asleep. But it didn't always work out that way. Sometimes I had to do it during late afternoon or early evening, when my husband unexpectedly was working late. The most frustrating thing was when he came home at a critical point of the game—such as right in the middle of the buy two-get-one-free pages. You see, he didn't know about my catalogs and our special games. So, he would say, "What have you been doing all day?"

I may not always have been truthfully able to answer, "Cooking, cleaning, and child-rearing, all day long," like a

good little housewife should. But I never implicated my
secret friends, the catalogs, either.

On those evenings when he'd come home unexpectedly,
right in the middle of our time together, I'd run and hide in
the bathroom. When he banged on the door, I would plead
digestion difficulties and beg him not to open the door. All
the while, I furiously added up my prices, as fast as I could,
until I reached one thousand. Then, I'd hide the catalog and
calmly emerge to see what everyone needed me to do.

I know how it must sound. But try to understand—a
young mother living out in the middle of nowhere needs to
have her fun.

The Dishes

I never liked doing the dishes. Washing my own dishes
is okay because I usually rinse them right after using them,
so nothing gets crusted on and needs hard scrubbing later.
Ever since, I was nine years old, though, I had to wash other
people's dishes, which were usually encrusted with Velvee-
ta and surrounded by floating bread crusts, cigarette butts,
and cellophane juice-box wrappers.

The only way I could stand to do it was with the radio on,
because the music soothed the savage dishwashing beast. If I
was alone, I would sing along to the songs in harmony or
counterpoint and sometimes dance a little with just my hips
or my shoulders while the water swished around. When I
couldn't listen to my radio because it would be turned off in
in favor of the TV, I would resort to fantasy.

The fantasies were usually about rock stars. But sometimes they were about other things, too. Like how weirdly
different my life would have been if I'd finished school
instead of dropping out to start a family. Or how life would
be in a real city or town, instead of in the middle of nowhere.
Or how it would feel to have friends.

Something about the mechanical wetness makes fantasizing easy. I lingered over the suds, making the most of my sinkside sentence.

Keeping in Touch

Dear Letty,

We got a new van. It's large. It used to be a daycare bus. It's solid white. The kids love it because they can each have their own bench seat. It has AC vents all along the headliner.

The old van has to sit in the back yard now. It cries a little at night but I just scream "Shut up, damn you!" out the window at it. No one likes that stinky, sweaty, striped van anymore. No one likes a whiner.

Just kidding.

Last week I was thinking that I wanted to write a poem about Spiderman. I wanted to talk about his relationship with his wife because I always thought that the way he neglected her was shameful.

Now, however, I wonder why she never left him. Was the secret prestige of being Spiderman's wife just too irresistible? Did she feel that she deserved to live that way? Could she think of nothing better to do with her life than sitting around waiting for her jerk husband to get home?

So I went to a couple of comic book web sites to do some research. I found out that Mary Jane, Spiderman's wife, had grown up in a dysfunctional family. Before she hooked up with Spidey, she had all the classic man-needing issues suffered by women with low self-esteem.

So now I don't feel like making fun of her anymore.

I need to take a nap. I stayed up pretty late last night, thinking about Spiderman and important stuff like that.

Everything else is the same. Nothing new.

Write me back, okay?

Recreation, Part I

I didn't like camping, but I'd go along anyway to prove my love and devotion to my family.

I think trailer trash people like camping because it gives them a chance to escape from their trailers for a while and be a little freer out in the wild. While I certainly could have appreciated that motivation, I was too distracted by the bug-infested showers and fish-smelling dumpsters to discover it at that time.

During our long drives to the campsites, we'd pass towns even smaller and duller than the one that contained our own sky-blue trailer. Although I hated our small town, I would look out the window and imagine what life would be like if we moved farther out in the Middle of Nowhere.

I would fantasize that I was an important part of the alternate small town community. I would run a shop that sold exciting new things to the bored housewives. Things to enliven their lives. I would make our trailer into a retro-swanky palace and hosted soirees that had all the neighbors hoping for invitations. "There's Gwen. Hi, Gwen!" people would say as I walked down the street.

Something was *wrong* with our particular small town, I realized. Somehow, it kept me from doing anything at all.

Recreation, Part II

I liked to go to the karaoke bars because, before I became trailer trash, I used to sing. I sang Broadway musicals in a little performing arts troupe, songs of my own composition in a crappy little rock band, and whole Catholic masses at the neighborhood church. I even studied opera for a while. The only thing I'd never really sung was country.

Once we drove by a ratty little bar, or "watering hole," as it proclaimed itself to be, and I noted a sign that said "KARAOKE HERE: MON, WED, FRI". I begged my hus-

band to take me there. Eventually, he did. We went to cele-brate our anniversary.

There were about 500 songs on the KJ's list, and most of them were country. I managed to find "Bewitched," an old standard I knew pretty well. But I was too nervous to sign up to sing. Bothered and bewildered, my husband drove us home.

Although I had been on stage many, many times in my youth and had always loved the attention and the applause, something had changed. I didn't have my old confidence anymore. My voice was out of shape, for one thing. But, also, I wondered what people would think. "Who the hell is this frumpy chick, and why do we wanna hear her sing?"

The other trailer trash women, frumpy or not, seemed to have no such hesitation. They fell into three main types: those who sang in Baptist choirs and were proud to show off their God-given talent, those who obviously practiced for hours each day until their voices were indistinguishable from Patsy Cline's, and those who were too drunk to care what they sounded like. Most of them took advantage of the KJ's $5 recording service and went home with taped memorials of their successes.

We went back to the bar on subsequent occasions. Eventually, an amaretto sour gave me the courage to choke out song. The KJ whispered basic vocalization techniques with his hand over his microphone. "Breath! Sing Louder!" Shamefully, I imagined what any of my old voice coaches would have said if they'd seen.

All the way home I sang the song as I should have, anger and determination giving me back my voice. "Okay, that's enough," my husband finally said.

The next time we went, it was my twenty-six or twenty-seventh birthday. We'd dropped our three kids off at my mother-in-law's for the evening and I was ready to make the most of it. After two amaretto sours, I slammed the big book open to my dream karaoke song, "Last Dance," by Her

Disco Highness, Donna Summers.

"I don't think these people are gonna wanna hear that," my husband said.

"I don't care," I replied. I put my name on the list and, before I had time to chicken out, it was my turn.

I got up on stage and told myself that *this* was *my* last chance. Last dance, last chance for love. I sang my freaking heart out. Everyone in the bar hooted, whistled, and danced. I nailed the high note so beautifully, the KJ played it back on his recorder for everyone to hear again.

Strangers congratulated and complimented me as I made my way back to my husband's pool table. Then a little man in a big black cowboy hat got up and belted out something by the Village People. Then someone else sang something by the Bee Gees. We all danced together. I had shown them the magic of disco. For one night, I had touched their lives.

I glowed with pride all the way through the next pool game and then through our meal at the International House of Pancakes.

Throughout the years that followed, I reminisced about that night and looked forward to the next time that I'd have that much fun.

Day-to-Day

All the feminist literature I'd read in college had warned against the entrapment of housewifery. Nonetheless, I'd decided to stay home with the kids until they were old enough to go to school. I'd had bad experiences at daycare centers when I was a child, and I wanted my kids to have better childhoods than mine. The women who'd written the feminist books didn't understand my culture. I was nineteen years old. I knew what I was doing.

Housework was heinous and I did as little of it as I could get away with. My kids were fabulous and I did as much as I could to show them my love. Boredom was inevitable and

I fought it with everything at my disposal. Here is what I did over the next few years:

- Gardened.
- Sewed.
- Dropped out of college.
- Crocheted doilies.
- Baked bread.
- Developed weird little obsessions.
- Made piñatas for my kids' birthdays.
- Taught the kids to dance to Mexican music, just in case we ever went back to my hometown and danced like I used to before I got married.
- Fought with my husband until I cried.
- Drove the kids to soccer practice.
- Took the kids to the library.
- Held my kids in my arms until they fell asleep, and then I cried.
- Gathered pecans, shelled them, and made pecan pies.
- Spread newspapers all over the dining room table and taught the kids to paint.
- Visited my mother-in-law.
- Yelled at my kids and spanked them. Then I cried.
- Killed ants and roaches.
- Fed stray cats.
- Taught myself to use my husband's computer.
- Taught my kids to make prank calls.
- Told my husband I had to go to the drugstore to buy feminine hygiene products, then I drove around the edges of town, listening to the radio and crying.
- Watched TV. Trailer trash people watch a lot of TV.

Recreation, Part III

Late at night, on my husband's computer, I discovered the miracle of the Internet.

The Internet was a way to reach out to people who were far away. People who couldn't see you. People who could only judge you by your words.

Weirdly, people seemed to like my words sometimes. My words could somehow make them pay attention.

I got a thrill out of typing words that people liked to read—out of fooling people into believing that I was someone worth listening to.

I typed words late at night. I slept late in the morning. This wasn't behavior becoming of a trailer trash housewife. But, come on, even trailer trash housewives need to have some fun.

The Fights

What's a trailer trash marriage without fighting? All blue-collar couples fight. You learn that from TV.

Here are the rules for fighting on TV:

1. Snide remarks mask true love.
2. Issues are resolved within 24 minutes.
3. The winner is the one who makes the audience laugh the most.

Here are the rules for fighting in real life:

1. The rules of logic don't apply.
2. The winner is the one who controls the money.
3. The cops can't do anything until you actually get hit.

Have fun, lovebirds!

Lessons Learned

All my weird little obsessions with catalogs and crossword puzzles and q-tips and the like became one big obsession with putting my writing and my drawings on the Internet and gathering all the applause I could. I got writing jobs.

I made friends. I saved money from my jobs and traveled to meet those friends. I talked to those friends on the phone late at night, when everyone else was asleep. As you can imagine, that didn't leave me as much time to garden, sew or bake pies. Or to cook or clean.

Suddenly, I wasn't a trailer trash housewife at all. I had deserted my post. The center could not hold. The space-time continuum was disrupted. All hell broke loose.

So, I left. And nothing has been the same since.

One important thing I learned from my experience is that, if the world were suddenly to become a sea of multi-colored trailers tethered to cement, buoyed on beer cans and proudly flying American flags assembled in Taiwan, then I would be able to survive.

The most important thing I learned was that, no matter what happens, I'm going to survive, anyway.

Fiction Is good Because It Lets You Pretend You're Lying

Crazy Tony

*T*ina found out her cousin was out of jail when she heard him call her name. Coming out of Happy Land with her grandmother's Coke and sunflower seeds in a brown paper bag, she's careful to keep her face turned from the drunks who habitually stand in front of the little store. Although they're mostly harmless, neighborhood boys ranging in age from seventeen to forty three, it's best not to attract their attention, ever.

"Hey, Tina!"

She turns with a wince.

There among the literal usual suspects—Crazy Tony, fat Beto, one-armed Jaime, glue-sniffing George, prematurely graying Lalo—is her cousin Rudy. His eyes are already dilated. From what, Tina doesn't know. His constant leer twists his face, and his sharp elbows and fingers jut in all directions as he stares at her with his mouth open, spit ejecting itself from his lips. Tina thinks of a dog she saw the day before that seemed to smile as it ate dirty diapers from a dumpster

"Hey," she says in greeting, wondering how he got out of jail and back to the neighborhood without her grandmother knowing about it ahead of time.

"Hey, Tina . . . Crazy Tony here wants to ask you a question!"

Surprised, Tina and the others turn to Crazy Tony, who

seems most surprised of all. His face, which always twitches and jerks on its own, twitches faster than usual and turns red.

"Wha-wha-what, man? I didn't—I . . ."

"That's all right, man. You tell her later, when y'all two are alone!"

Rudy laughs like a jackal.

Great, Tina thinks, just what I need: another pervert after me. She turns her face to the street and follows it home.

$\approx\infty$

There are a lot of people in the neighborhood who get called crazy. Crazy Victor, Crazy Lupe, Crazy Susie on Kane Street. Some of them really are mentally ill, but some aren't. Crazy Victor's just mentally retarded and he holds his hands weird when he walks. Crazy Lupe's speech is slurred, so you can't tell if he's saying crazy things or just regular stuff. People say he got hit by a train one night while running from the cops, and it scrambled his brains.

Tina used to lie about Crazy Susie being her mom. She would tell people her mother was dead. Everyone pretended to believe it, for her sake. As if Crazy Susie had just happened to pick Tina's front yard to yell from for no reason at all. As if Tina's grandmother was just too charitable to call the cops unless Susie got really violent, waving a tree branch and screaming.

"Get away from me! I'm not gonna let you rape me again, you dirty motherfuckers!"

Normally, though, Susie just walks the neighborhood streets and around downtown, hauling a little bag of clothes and staring at people. Sometime she gets hungry enough to go back to Tina's tan brick house and accept a bean taco or boloney sandwich from Tina's grandmother, who used to be her mother-in-law.

Tina sleeps over with friends a lot. One night, during a

game of Truth or Dare, she found out that her friends and everybody else had known about Crazy Susie being her mom all along. At first she'd been embarrassed, but now it's just one less thing to worry about.

Mrs. Hernández, in the big orange house down the street, had given birth to five boys. With that many, it wasn't surprising that two of them would turn out to be crazy. People say that Crazy Danny, her youngest, would take puppies up the Dow School fire slide and do nasty things to them. He went to jail when he was eighteen. Tina doesn't know why.

His brother, Crazy Tony, seems normal, except for his face. His eyes blink a lot and the corner of his mouth jerks up sometimes, as if he's trying to stop thinking about something funny but gross. If it weren't for that, he'd almost be good-looking, like his older brothers. He doesn't have a job. But, then, Tina's cousin Rudy doesn't either, and they dropped out of school the same year.

Tony doesn't talk a lot. He walks the streets all day in his camouflage jacket, or else he drinks beer with the guys in front of Happy Land. People say he freaks out sometimes. Tina's never seen it.

Tina feels bad for Mrs. Hernández. She knows what a pain in the butt it can be to have crazy people in your family. But at the same time, she sometimes thinks that having drunks and drug addicts is just as bad.

⁖∎

Sometimes hanging out with the drunks and the drug addicts in front of the red store gets kind of old, even for Tony. He crushes his Bud can. "Later, man," and "Tell Manuel I said what's up," they say as he walks away, through the vacant lot, towards Washington Avenue.

Really, it's almost time to go home, but he wants to walk for a while, first. He crosses over to the Salvation Army and heads west.

Rudy's back. Not like you could miss it, with the way he talks so loud and puts his hand on everybody's shoulder all the time. Asking people if they're fags. Bragging about some chick he claims to have screwed the week before.

Tony wonders if his brother knows that Rudy's out and what he'll do when he finds out. Rudy was working for Manuel when he got busted. Manuel had been ready to get rid of him, anyway, because Rudy was a big mouth and a thief. Then, he didn't have to worry about it anymore because Rudy got himself caught way out in Magnolia trying to cut deals with some guys nobody ever heard of. He knew better than to say Manuel's name to the cops, though. Manuel doesn't play that.

Tony walks almost all the way to Studewood, past all the car lots and hubcap lots and the tombstone place. He stops outside the gate of the big cemetery so he can look at the trees.

☜∘☞

When Tony gets home, his mom is talking on the phone and watching the news from her place on the living room couch.

"Here's Tony. He looks hungry. I got them some ham to make sandwiches," she says, gesturing towards the kitchen with her cigarette.

Tony steps between the table holding his mom's ashtray, Coke and phone and the table holding her cigarettes, lighter and newspapers to give her a kiss on the cheek. She takes it with a drag on her Winston Light. He steps over her phone cord and lamp cord on his way to the kitchen.

"Manuel should be home soon," he hears her tell her friend. "Oh, my God—they *did* shoot him—you were right, Chela!"

She's talking about someone who got shot on the news—not someone real. Tony sits at the little yellow kitchen table with his sandwich and the last can of Coke.

"Oh, here comes Manuel down the street."

Tony chews the bread and pushes crumbs around he paper plate.

"Here he comes up the steps."

Tony watches a squirrel through the kitchen window.

"He just came through the door."

Tony takes the last drink of his Coke.

"He gave me a hundred dollars grocery money and two cartons of cigarettes. He's such a good boy."

Tony very quietly burps.

Manuel walks into the kitchen. His black hair, wiry but all pushed into the same direction, almost scrapes the light bulb hanging from the wires in the middle of the ceiling.

"Hey, man," he says.

Tony nods.

"You know Rudy's back?"

"Yeah," says Tony.

Manuel nods. He takes his cigarettes from the pocket of his black Members Only jacket and waves them at Tony, who waves no, thanks.

He smokes his cigarette. He looks out the window, at the picture of the Aztec princess on his mother's wall calendar and then at nothing at all. Tony picks the food from his teeth and wipes it on a paper towel.

Manuel stubs out his cigarette in the big conch-shaped ashtray that serves as the table's centerpiece.

"You wanna go see if mom needs anything from the store before *MASH* comes on?"

Tony nods.

"You need anything? You need any money?"

Tony shakes his head. "Nah, man, thanks."

"All right, man. I gotta take off. Take it easy, all right?"

"All right, man. Take it easy," says Tony.

He watches the clean-cut back of his brother's neck and then the shininess of his shoes as Manuel goes back out the door, back to work.

೧೦೯

Tina unties the green and red flowered sheet stapled above her window, blocking the view from the street. Then she turns on her radio. It sits on the nightstand with the lamp and the Barbie whose hair has been permanent-marker-ed sultry black. She adjusts the tuning knob, careful not to disturb the masking tape holding the radio's batteries in. She's able to bring in a popular dance song; strong enough on its own that she can let go of thee radio and take a tentative step back, like a mother watching her toddler stand on his own.

Tina stands still for a while, listening.

Last week, her school held a homecoming dance. She didn't go. But if she had gone, she probably would have danced. She half-closes her eyes to picture it better, sees herself spinning and undulating in a watermelon-pink satin dress.

The index finger of her right hand taps against her thigh.

She would have worn high heels and tossed her hair so it rippled with the rest of her body. She would have thrown her arms in the air.

The shadow of her, on the wall, is much larger than life. Even so, the twitches of her hips are barely detectable. Back and forth, the tiniest bit, steady to the music.

"Hey, girl! What are you doing in here?"

Tina shrieks as she spins around, knocking he radio off the nightstand so that one of its batteries tumbles out and rolls under the tattered pink bed.

Rudy laughs loudly, as if he just watched someone fall down on TV.

"What do you want?" she says, crossing her arms in front of her chest to stop its heat from shooting into her face.

"Nothing. I just came to see if you were in here writing love letters."

Tina's lip curls but she can't think of anything to say to this. Rudy takes a step forward, forcing her to take a step back.

"I thought you were gonna be writing love letters to your new boyfriend, but you're doin' a little dance for him, instead."

"No, I wasn't."

"Yeah, you were. What are you gonna do for him, huh?"

Rudy moves forward again. Tina leans back as far as she can towards the nightstand and the wall.

"What are y'all doing in here?"

Rudy whips around and, at the same time, takes all his steps backwards again in one big jump. Then he sees that it's only Eddie, Tina's younger brother. The smart ass.

"Shut up, punk. None of your business."

"You shut up," says Eddie.

"Say what, man? What'd you say?"

Eddie looks into Rudy's eyes, or at a spot between them, and doesn't look away.

Rudy turns to Tina, whose eyes are wide on her brother, and then laughs. "Man, you're lucky I don't feel like kicking your ass right now."

He pushes past Eddie and ruffles his hair hard enough to shove his head forward and then back again.

"Man, fuck you!?" says Eddie.

He turns to slap Rudy's arm away, too late to hit it very hard. Rudy quickly turns back and slaps Eddie lightly on the face.

"Man, fuck you!" he mimics. "Watch your mouth, boy!"

Eddie swings a fist at him and just misses as Rudy jumps away again, now hopping on his toes like a boxer on speed and, of course, still laughing. Eddie balls both fists and stays where he is.

"Asshole. Why don't you go back to jail with your dad?"

Rudy gets still. "Say that to my face, faggot."

"You heard me."

Just like in her dreams, Tina is frozen, only able to watch, not to scream. But, just like in her dreams, she can eventually whisper. *Quit it . . .*

And then she talks. "Quit it . . . ."

And then, finally, she wakes up and yells for help. "Quit it! Quit! Grandma!"

Her grandmother's already shuffling down the hall. "What in the hell are y'all making all this noise for?"

Tina says nothing. Eddie says nothing. Their brown eyes are matching blanks in their faces.

"Nothing, Grandma," says Rudy.

"Don't you nothing me. I heard y'all fighting."

Tina sees her youngest brother Jesse standing in the hall, watching.

"Shoot, I don't know," says Rudy. "I just came up here to tell Tina she needed to go help you with dinner. Then this little punk came in and started trying to hit me for nothing."

Their grandmother looks at them, one by one. Tina and Eddie still say nothing.

"Well . . . Well, y'all better behave. Unless you want me to get the broom on y'all." She shuffles towards the door. "And, Tina, I do need you to help me. Come on."

The minute she disappears around the corner, Rudy slaps Eddie across the top of the head. "Y'all better behave." He turns and lightly runs out after their grandmother, giggling.

Eddie is breathing hard enough for Tina to hear. She swallows hard and doesn't cry. Jesse practically hisses.

"I hate that motherfucker! Let's go get him, Eddie, when he gets in his room," says Jesse, his voice not even breaking. His eleventh birthday was the week before.

"Nah, man. Nah," says Eddie. "He's just a punk. Forget his stupid ass."

He stands still for a while, visibly becoming calm, then turns to Tina. "How come you don't have a lock on your door?"

"A lock? I don't know," she says.

He goes away, Jesse following. He comes back with a hammer and a thin block of wood about a half foot long.

"You got a nail?" he asks his sister.

Tina crosses the room to where a defunct sink sits on a cabinet in the corner. She yanks open one of the cabinet drawers, which has become stiff with many layers of pain and humidity, and finds a long rusted nail.

Eddie takes it from her hand. He goes to her room door, closes it and hammers the block of wood into the molding at its side. He swivels the wood, across the door, and then counterclockwise up again.

"There's your lock," he says. He leaves the room. Jesse, who's been waiting, follows.

❧

"Check this out, man. Check it out!"

"Aw . . . Damn. Where'd you get that, man?"

Tony takes a sip of his beer and pushes away the crumpled magazine nudging his arm. It's opened to a picture of a naked chick doing something nasty with a banana. Rudy brought it to the store in a brown paper bag, and he's handing it around for all the guys to see. Tony doesn't touch it. He doesn't want to know where it's been.

"Hey, man . . . Look what else I got," says Rudy.

He sticks his hand in the paper bag and pulls out some weed, holding it close so the kids and old ladies passing by won't see it, even if they hear him talking about it loud as hell.

"Aw, man!" says Chuy, who's not even old enough to buy his own beer.

"Hell, yeah. Check this shit out. This isn't the same old shit from Manuel . . . I found out a way to make it better."

Tony knows Rudy's lying, but he doesn't care enough to argue about it.

"Come on, man. Let's go to the lot and roll a joint."

Rudy puts the weed back in the bag along with his magazine.

"All right, man."

"Hell, yeah!"

They head towards the empty lot two blocks down that's conveniently outfitted with vine-swarmed trees and an abandoned couch.

"You coming Tony?"

"Nah, man. I got stuff to do."

"Yeah, man, let him go. He gots stuff to do. Like jerking off!" says Rudy, laughing and slapping Tony's arm.

Tony pushes his hand away. "Hey, man . . . I already told you. I don't play that shit."

The other guys stop laughing. Their tones and faces are somber as they say, "Hey, man" and "Come on, man" and "Come on, Tony man." Rudy tones his cackling down to a smile.

"Yeah, man, Tony. Why you gotta get mad? Come on, man."

"It's cool," says Tony. And so it is cool, and they let him take off.

☜❦☞

It hasn't rained in a while so it's too humid to walk around. Tony goes home, thinking he'll watch *Donahue* with his mom. When he reaches his empty house, he remembers his mother talking to her friend the night before about getting a ride to the doctor's.

He goes to the kitchen and looks in the refrigerator, then takes out the ham and the cheese and sets them on the counter. He picks at his teeth for a moment.

He goes to the bathroom. Then, he goes to the room that he used to share with Manuel and Danny and sits on the edge of the bottom bunk. He chews his nails for a while. He spits out his results and lies down.

That picture of the chick with the banana was pretty disgusting. Normally, he doesn't think about stuff like that, but sometimes you can't help yourself.

His legs are jittering and his eye is twitching worse than usual. Finally he gives up, reaches for a dirty t-shirt on the floor behind his head and then unzips his jeans.

The stupid banana chick was obviously high. Worse than that, though, she won't stay still in his mind. First she's herself, with the weasel-looking face. Then, her face turns to Rosario's from down the street. Rosario in torn, short shorts. Then she's someone else altogether: someone else in a pair of jeans. The back of those jeans, walking away from him. Just the other day. Tight jeans. No, it's not Rudy's cousin. She's too young.

It must have been Rosario's jeans. She walks by Happy Land about five times a day.

"Stupid!" she says when the guys whistle at her. "*Stoopid!*"

Actually, they said she's pregnant now. So he can't think about her anymore.

There's the girl who works at Happy Land. She's nice, but sort of scary at the same time, with her black eyes, lips and nails. Not her either, then.

Sweating now, Tony thinks of the banana chick and does what he has to do. Her face flickers like a slide show and transforms from one girl's to another's. When he's finally done, he feels the beer messing up his stomach. He makes himself go spit in the sink.

࿐

Tina helps with dinner, like always. Her grandmother shuffles through the kitchen, muttering.

"You shouldn't spend the night at Melissa's house so much. Her mother probably wishes you'd go home. You spent the whole weekend there. I need you here, helping me.

I'm getting too old to do everything by myself."

Tina chops pickles. The old lady shuffles to her room to answer the phone. At the same time, the front door bangs open and slams shut. Tina hopes it isn't Rudy, but knows it is.

"Hey, I just saw Crazy Tony. He says he wants to meet you tonight by the store. I told him you would go."

He moves closer to Tina. She turns so that the big bowl she's holding is between them.

"Grandma, did you want me to put pepper in the tuna fish?" she calls.

Her grandmother's still talking on the phone.

"I told him you'd go see him because you're always going to see your boyfriends at night. Beto told me he saw you and your little friend at Studewood Park with two guys. He said y'all had on short little skirts and shirts with no bras. . . ."

He leans as close to her face as he can in order to say this last part softly. His hands move forward, floating on either side of her like hot, sweaty blimps. She leans back as far as she can against the stove.

Her grandmother comes through the sheet that hangs between her bedroom and the kitchen.

"Here . . . let me taste it and see."

Rudy calmly stands up straight, takes a pickle off the cutting board and eats it. His grandmother slaps his hand.

"A little bit more pepper. That's all. What are you doing home, *m'ijo*? I thought you were going to see Manuel."

"I did, Grandma. I'm gonna start working with him again. He said he's been waiting for me to come back, since I'm the only one he can trust to drive his delivery truck."

"Well, that's good," their grandmother says. "That's what I figured."

"As soon as I get my first paycheck, I'm gonna go to the flea market and get you that ashtray I was telling you about . . . the marble one from Japan with the Virgin Mary on it."

Tina turns back to her cooking. She's glad Rudy will be out dealing again, no matter what he tells their grandmother.

❧

It's Monday morning, so everyone in the house is asleep, except for Tina. Her brothers have been gone since dark. Whether they went to school or not, she doesn't know.

Her grandmother never wakes up when Tina sneaks into her bedroom, a room that could almost be considered pretty. In the bathroom, faded roses surround her. Tina reaches across all the dusty toiletries on the bureau to take the bottle of Emeraude. Muffling it with her t-shirt, she sprays a tiny bit down at her stomach, where she can be sure no one will smell it. This ritual complete, she gazes into the smoky mirror.

She examines her chin, forehead and the corners behind her nostrils. She runs her hands through her hair, then gathers it all on top of her head. She purses her lips and raises one brow and then the other.

The light coming through the room's tiny, whitewashed window shows that there's still a bit of time before the bus comes. Tina crouches down and slides open the bottom bureau drawer.

Under the embroidered handkerchiefs and buttoned gloves that no one will ever use again, there's a very small amount of makeup. Tina ignores the crusted black pancake of mascara, the stale-smelling pancake of "pancake" and the siren song of the blue eye shadow that has gotten her in trouble before. Her fingers go directly to the tiny sample tube of Avon Pink Sails lipstick. This morning, she will be brave.

The lipstick is the exact color of her lips. But something about it makes her face different in the mirror. Her chin tilts and her eyes wink knowingly all on their own. Tina slips out of her grandmother's room and then out the front door.

❧

On the way to the bus stop, hugging her books to her chest, Tina imagines what Melissa will say. Her parents never let her wear makeup. Poor Melissa. She'll be very, very jealous.

All of a sudden, Tina sees a cat.

She jaywalks across the street to the bus stop near the old fire station, where the tabby cat is rubbing its chin against a bent corner of the garage door. It looks up as she arrives, pupils dilating against the morning sun. Tina gets all the way up to it and then bends down and extends her hand. The cat minces away, slipping through the space between the fire station and the chain-link fence surrounding the neighboring weed-filled lot.

"Aw . . . come on, kitty. Here, kitty, kitty," Tina calls.

It watches with narrowed eyes. She reaches for its face through the fence.

A car honks behind her, but Tina doesn't notice. She stretches her fingers through one of the fence's pewter diamonds and touches a single whisker. The cat never takes a step back, but its somehow able to pull its head a remarkable distance away without seeming to move at all.

"Hey," says a man's voice. Tina spins around to see who's there. It's a bald business man in an old blue Buick, idling right there at the bus stop sign.

"Good morning. You're looking real pretty today. Need a ride?"

Tina averts her eyes, looking toward the neon bail bonds signs in the distance. There's a lot of traffic, so the man is forced to drive on. Relieved, she turns back to the cat. It's gone. She sighs and turns back towards the street, leaning her back against the fire station wall. It looks like she missed the 7:55. She'll have to wait for the 8:06 now.

After a while, the blue Buick comes back.

"Where are you going? To school? Get in and I'll give you a ride."

The man is leaning far across the bench seat to peer at her out of his passenger-side window, ready to open the door.

Again, Tina looks down the street as if she doesn't hear him.

"Come on. Get in."

She stares steadily down the street, waiting for the bus to come around the corner three blocks away.

The car behind the Buick honks and the man has to drive on again. Out of the corner of her eye, Tina sees him turn the corner to come around the block again. She squints down the avenue to her left, eyes watering. She can almost see . . . she sees it. Here's the bus.

Also, here's Crazy Tony.

He's coming towards her. A block away.

Tina strains her eyes to read the lighted name on the top of the bus as it effortlessly catches up with Tony and then passes him by. H . . . A . . . Wrong one. It passes her, too.

Tony comes closer and closer. He's walking quickly, with his hands in his pockets. He's looking down at the cracked sidewalk, but Tina can see that his lips are moving continuously. He's talking to himself. She steps back into the four inches of shelter provided by the recess of the fire station's garage door, flattening her back against it.

Meanwhile, the blue Buick is cruising up to the bus stop once again. No one's behind it this time, so the bald man comes to a complete stop. He leans towards the passenger-side window again and opens his mouth to speak. But Tina speaks first.

"Look, I don't want a damned ride, okay?"

The man shuts his mouth. He's silent for a second, staring at her. Tina looks at a yellow stain on his blue-stripped tie.

When he finally speaks, it's loud. "Hey, you little bitch. Who do you think you are? Someone needs to teach you some manners."

Tina decides to go back to ignoring him.

He talks louder. "I'm over here trying to be a gentleman, offering a ride to a little slut like you. The least you could do is say thank you. Do you hear me? I ought to get out of this car and slap your little face."

Tina looks away to the right, eyes stinging.

Crazy Tony's reached the bus stop by now. He might have heard the whole thing. She puts her hand up to her mouth, fights the urge to completely cover her face.

But Tony doesn't seem to have noticed anything. The man twists in his seat to look at him, and Tina considers taking the opportunity to run away. Her hands fall to her sides. Her legs tense.

"Look, why don't you just get in the car and I won't be mad."

By then Tony has gotten close enough for Tina to hear that he isn't talking to himself. He's quietly singing "Born in the USA." But now he stops singing, stops walking and looks at the man, who says to Tina, "You coming or not?"

Tony looks at Tina as if he's just noticed her standing there.

"Tina, is this guy messing with you?"

She looks down at her feet.

"Hey, man, are you messing with her?"

"Nobody's messing with anyone. This young lady just asked me for a ride."

Tony stares at the man for about five seconds.

"Get out of here. She don't play that shit, man. I don't play that shit either. Get out of here."

The guy opens his mouth as if to say something, but then instead moves back to the driver's seat, puts the car in gear, and takes off, yelling "You're crazy!"

Tina is left alone with Crazy Tony.

There's a long silence. She doesn't look to see if he's

still looking at her. Eventually, she remembers the manners her grandmother taught her.

"Thanks."

"Tina, you need to be careful. There's some messed-up guys around here."

"Yeah, well . . . thanks."

The bus pulls up with a loud squeal and a release of air. Tina hurries into it.

☜∾☞

Tony remembers Tina's face when that pervert was messing with her. Not just like she didn't want to be there, but like she wasn't there. Like she just spaced out and went somewhere else in her mind. Good thing that guy was just a punk who wouldn't really do anything. Tony's seen him before, trying to pick up girls at all the bus stops from here to 20th.

It's the afternoon of that same day. He's sitting at the drugstore counter, drinking a cherry Coke that he won't have to pay for because Neno, the old guy who runs the counter, wants to suck up to Tony's brother. Tony ignores the way Neno smiles at him every time he comes by with his dirty rag.

He thinks about Tina standing there trying to pet that stupid cat through the gate, and he has to laugh. She's just like Danny was—always trying to pet some damned animal. Always noticing some squirrel, bird, lizard. . . . She'd probably want to pet a baby alligator, if you let her.

And her face got like Danny's, too, when people told her shit. Scared and then blanked out—not there.

His dad picked on Danny most because he was the easiest. He'd call him a little faggot, and Danny wouldn't say anything, wouldn't even look mad. Then he'd hit Danny across the head and laugh when Danny still didn't do anything. Only a tear would leak down from his eye.

It's a good thing their father's gone. Everything's as

good as it can be for them now. Manuel's doing good, making money. Louis is in the Army and he's probably going to stay past the four years. Too bad Georgie's dead and Danny's where he is. But still, they're doing good. Tony used to wonder if he should leave, try to join the army, too. But instead, he keeps on staying with his mom. He doesn't want her to be alone and afraid.

Tony holds out a dollar to pay for his Coke. Neno waves it away, tries to put his hand on Tony's, but Tony pulls his back, first. He gets up to go, not having any plan as to where he'll actually be.

He used to wonder why his mom married an asshole like their father. Then he figured out that there probably just wasn't anybody else.

He thinks of all the guys who live in the neighborhood now. He hopes Tina moves away before it's too late.

෴

Two nights after the bus stop incident, Tina's in the kitchen with her grandmother.

"Grandma, do you know that guy Crazy Tony?"

"You mean Mrs. Hernández's boy?"

"Yeah."

"Don't call him Crazy like that. It's ugly."

"So, he's not crazy?" Tina wipes a bit of potato from the big spoon and licks her finger.

"Well . . . ." Her grandmother frowns, a small change from her normal expression. "Not crazy like your mother, no."

"So what happened to him?"

"I don't know for sure. You remember all that stuff that happened with his daddy? Well, they said it scrambled his brains."

"What stuff that happened with his dad?" Tina asks.

"Put some more mayonnaise. Not that much. That's good. Well . . . I guess you were too young to remember. His father used to come home drunk and hit him and his brothers and Mrs. Hernández. I heard he did other stuff, too, to the youngest boy. Nasty stuff."

"Like what?" Tina says, letting go of the spoon.

"You know . . . molested him. Or that's what they said. Who knows? You know how people are."

"So then what happened? Where's the dad now?"

"Smash up those eggs better," says her grandmother. "I don't like thick eggs in my potato salad. Nobody knows where he is. The oldest brother, Manuel, beat the heck out of him one night. Sometimes they say he killed him, but we would have heard the ambulance. Or the police. I think he just went off to live with some woman."

Tina stirred pickles, salt and pepper into the bowl, then covered it with plastic wrap.

"Grandma, do you think the dad molested Tony, too, and that's why they call him Crazy?"

"I don't know, *m'ija*. I couldn't tell you."

"Why do you think their dad was like that?" Tina says.

"I don't know *m'ija*. Well, probably because his father did it to him. The other day on *Donahue* they had women who had been sexually abused, and the doctor was saying that sometimes it happens like that—like a cycle. And that it happens all the time."

"Really?" Tina says. "Did it ever happen to you?"

"Of course," says her grandmother. "I had big boobs and big *nalgas*, like you. Men always wanted to touch them."

"But did it ever happen with somebody in your family?"

"Yes . . . with one of my uncles. When we were staying at his ranch in the summer, to pick blackberries." Her grandmother wrinkles her nose, waves her hand as if at a fly. "He was always sweaty . . . breathing on my neck. I hated the way he smelled."

Tina waits, but that's all she gets.

"So what happened? How did it end?"

"Well, I told him to quit it, of course. And then we moved back with my mother when the summer was over."

Tina frowns and picks at her thumbnail.

"*M'ija.* . . ."

"Yeah, Grandma?"

"*M'ija*, if any of the boys around here ever messes with you—or if the men do—tell me, okay? I'll put a stop to it."

Tina lets out the breath that she's been holding. She takes a bigger breath and opens her mouth to speak, but her grandmother beats her to it.

"Or, if you don't want to tell me, tell Rudy, and *he'll* put a stop to it."

Tina closes her mouth again.

"Rudy will beat the heck out of anybody who messes with you. He knows how to respect women. I raised that boy right."

❧

Tina doesn't feel like going home. It's humid outside, but at least there's a breeze, unlike in her house. She's walking around the streets. Melissa went to a church youth group meeting, so there's no use trying to hang out with her. Tina looks at all the trees that have bloomed in the last couple of weeks and the flowers and Virgin Mary's in Mrs. López's yard, and the bugs, the lizards, the earthworms . . .

There's a cat under a car. Tina calls to it. It meows and rubs its face against the tire. Tina reaches. It saunters out, but then quickly walks away.

"Aw, come on," she tells it.

It makes a quick figure 8 under her touch, then walks out of reach again. Tina tries to scratch its chin, but it just meows in a slightly alarmed way and pretends to try to bite her.

"You have to pet the body."

She looks up and sees Tony there.

"Huh?"

"They like it when you pet the body first, then the head."

Tina stands with her legs and arms crossed, looking down at the cat. She almost wants to try Crazy Tony's advice, but she wishes he wasn't there to see.

The cat walks towards him and crashes into his leg. He strokes it along the back. It arches its back against his hand, circles his legs. A boy hoots as he rides by on his bike and the cat bolts under the car again.

"I guess it didn't want you to pet the body, either," Tina says.

"Sometimes they don't," says Tony. He laughs a little.

"What am I gonna do, make it stand there and let me touch it? C'mere, kitty . . . . Nah. I don't want to piss it off. Those things can scratch the crap out of you."

Tina laughs. She looks at Tony, imagining him trying to stroke and kiss a cat that's scratching the crap out of him. She doesn't notice when the cat slinks away into Mrs. López's yard.

Tony sees her looking at him, smiling like that. He looks to see where the cat has gone, wiping his hand over his forehead. When he pulls his hand back down, she's still smiling. He tries to look her in the eyes, but doesn't know if he's smiling back at her or just twitching. He runs his hand through his hair.

"Uh . . . I . . . I gotta go. My mom . . . she . . ."

Goddamned stuttering. He quits before he embarrasses himself any more.

Tina watches him stumble over a stick as he walks away. She has to laugh again. He's not crazy. He's cute.

の・ふ

It's Sunday morning. Tina and her friend Melissa are walking to the house to get some clothes and records for that night. They discuss the upcoming school dance and the lies Melissa will have to tell her parents in order to go. Tina still hasn't decided whether she'll go or not. She'll have to ask her grandmother, who will have to ask her dad, if he's at home and awake. Her dad will probably say no.

They turn the corner next to Tina's house and see Manuel and Rudy yelling at each other in the middle of the street.

"I told you, Rudy . . ."

"Say that again, man! Say it to my face!"

Rudy, obviously high, shoves Manuel as hard as he can. Manuel doesn't fall back, just punches Rudy in the face, knocking him to the ground. Tina and Melissa stop at the edge of the yard, as enthralled as everyone watching from the windows up and down the street.

"Quit it! Quit it!" Tina's grandmother yells, running out the front door with a broom held business-side-up above her head.

Manuel turns to face her.

"You get out of here! Nobody messes with my grandson!" she yells at him, swinging her weapon as if to swat him like a roach.

Manuel pulls back under it, but doesn't turn away. She half-swats again, then holds the broom over her shoulder like a baseball bat, glaring at him.

"Mrs. Chávez, I'm sorry to do this in front of your house. I don't mean you any disrespect. But you have to understand . . . I gave Rudy a job and then he stole from me."

She stares at him, words rushing to her lips and then dying away.

"I don't play that, Mrs. Chávez. I don't take that from anybody."

Tina's grandmother sighs and puts the broom down at her side. Manuel looks down at the street respectfully.

Rudy struggles up from the cement.

"Fuck you, man! I'll kick your fucking ass, you asshole!"

"Rudy, go inside," says his grandmother.

"Nah, man . . . I'm gonna kill this motherfucker!"

"Rudy. Go inside," says his grandmother, taking the broom in both hands again.

Rudy goes inside, muttering. Everyone else is silent until the door closes behind him. Then Manuel gets into his Camaro and drives away.

Tina's grandmother waddles to the porch, and sets the broom next to her on the steps. She takes her cigarettes and lighter from the pocket of her housedress.

Tina bites her lip, not sure what to do or what to say to her friend. This is almost as bad as finding her mother here.

Not to Melissa, though.

"Oh, my God . . ." she whispers. "I am totally in love."

ھ∽ف

Once again, Tina has managed to avoid her own home for most of the weekend. But now it's Monday night and she's back in the kitchen, washing the dishes made dirty by all the men in the house.

Rudy pops out of his room like a stoned jack-in-the-box, as if he's been waiting for her to show up the whole time.

"Leave me alone," she says before he can say anything. But he doesn't hear. The words he was planning are already coming out of his mouth.

"I bet you though that was funny, huh, having your faggot boyfriend's brother start shit with me right there in front of Grandma, where I couldn't do nothing. I bet you and your little friend liked that shit, huh?"

Tina is standing at the cutting board. She feels heat run from the space behind her eyes all the way down her arm to her fingers, which twitch. There's a big fork somewhere under them in the water. Also, a big knife.

"I told you, leave me alone."

"I told him you were like that, you were just a little slut . . ."

"Shut the hell up, Rudy."

". . . Always trying to get the guys to whistle at you on the street. . . ."

That is it. Tina is pissed off now.

Why is she always a slut? The girls at school, the men on the street, the old ladies in front of the church—all whispering or even just yelling slut, tramp, bitch. Her own father getting drunk and crying that she's a whore.

There's Crazy Tina. She was a slut and it scrambled her brains.

Tina laughs.

She turns around, looks Rudy right in the face. "That's right, man. Now you better take off before I tell him to come kick your ass again."

"Yeah, I bet you would, you little bitch . . . Hey, man . . . What the . . . ?"

She pulls a little fork out of the water and holds it up like a dagger, with water dripping from her fist.

"Get out of here, Rudy, before I kill your ugly ass. I don't play that shit anymore. I'll stab you with this fork."

"What the hell? What are you, crazy?"

Their grandmother comes through the sheet, just waking up.

"What's going on here?"

"Nothing, Grandma. Rudy's trying to mess with me, but I told him to let me do my work."

"Leave her alone, Rudy. Go take out the trash."

"Aw, man. . . ."

He's gone.

Tina sighs. "He's always messing with me. I'm tired of it."

"Well . . .Well, don't let him, *m'ija*. Tell him to quit."

Her grandmother searches her pocket for her cigarettes. Tina takes the pack off the butcher block and hands it to her.

"Grandma, can I go to a dance next weekend? At the school, with Melissa and Adriana?"

"A dance? With boys?"

"Yes."

Her grandmother studies her critically.

Tina waits, fork hidden in her hands, eyes on her grand-mother's slippers.

The old woman lights her cigarette with a deep drag.

"Well . . . okay." She blows smoke into the air, fakes a casual cough. "Okay . . . I guess it's about time you got yourself a boyfriend."

❧

Tony's on his way down Washington Avenue. He's head-ing to Happy Land to have a beer with the guys. Now that Rudy's gone back to jail—breaking and entering—it's a mellow place to hang out again.

The Number 50 bus pulls up alongside him. The doors open and out comes Tina, pushing her hair back with a hand as she steps down onto the curb. She looks up and sees him there.

"Tony! Hi."

"Hey," he tells her. "How's it going."

The bus pulls away. She looks at him and laughs. "It's going good."

Tony looks at the cars and billboards around them, but can't think of anything else to say. She's still smiling. And staring at him.

Then she laughs again. What the hell's so funny?

She smiles at him harder and stares into his face with a weird look in her eyes and one of her eyebrows kind of sticking up. Tony doesn't want to stare back. Maybe she has a tic. Then . . .

"Bye," she says in a weird kind of high-pitched voice. "I'll see you around, okay?"

She waves at him over her shoulder as she walks out into the avenue, cutting around the cars. He watches her make her way into the neighborhood, smiling, singing to herself, tossing her head.

Crazy.

He puts his hands in his pockets and goes on following the street.

Reina Cucaracha

Rosa Villarosa dances through the kitchen with her broom. The dishes, floors, stove, counters, walls, sink, table, chairs are all clean. Before moving on to the floors, tables, couches, curtains, windows, shelves, knick-knacks, and mirrors in the other rooms, there's a little time to dance.

The broom is a dashing *salsadero*, a pretty merengue man. He twirls Rosa around the floor. Her housedress swirls against her knees like silk, and the balls of her feet click-click in *chanclas* that, for all their light adeptness, might be the finest Italian leather.

Then—*ay*—another one runs across the counter. Up comes the broom. Down goes the broom.

Chihuahua, another on the floor. Down, hard down goes the broom.

Chinelas, these roaches! Whack, whack! goes the broom.

"Why must they bother me?" sighs Señora Villarosa. Didn't she just clean this kitchen? What will Jaime say, if he ever comes home tonight? How clean can a kitchen possibly be and still have roaches running and flying around?

With a spanking white dishtowel to her temple, Rosa Villarosa turns around and—*¡Dios mío!*—sees the hugest roach of all. The hugest roach she's ever seen in her whole entire life, standing right there in her kitchen, looking her right in the face.

"*Ay*" she says. Her eyes roll up to the Virgin, and she hopes her broom will catch her when she faints.

"No, Señora. Don't go away from me," says his voice. It's big and deep, mellifluous like Ricardo Montalbán yet shining like a chainsaw, this big, big cockroach's voice. "Señora Villarosa, don't go away so soon. I have come a long way to see you."

"Ah," she suddenly knows, "he is the King of the Roaches."

Looking again, she sees the extreme brilliance of his wing cloak, the bronze strength in his many appendages, and the royal, authoritative carriage of his—his head, that must be. Are those his eyes? Yes, that part there is moving with the voice—must be his face.

"Señora, put down your weapon. My minions have withdrawn and will bother you no more. Please, Doña Rosa, I ask that you tolerate my unworthy presence and grant me the gift of a few moments of your time."

With those tones, something awakens within her. This ain't no damned *borracho* in a work shirt, standing around kissing six packs with his *compadres*. This here is a gentleman.

Rosa wipes the fright from her face. With the innate grace native of her foremothers, she inclines her head, giving him permission to plead his case.

"Night after night, I send the subjects of my kingdom to see you—to spy on you, I admit, Señora Villarosa. I reach toward you, through them, so that I may see you dance."

Rosa nods as if she knew it all along, was used to this sort of thing, and was compassionate enough to give pardon to such impertinence.

The king continued, "Do you think that we come to you in order to steal the crumbs of your tortillas, wholesomely exquisite as they may be? Do we come to sip drops of Kool-Aid stirred so gracefully by your slender hand? No . . . No, Señora. I send my people to your sparkling kitchen so that, through their many eyes, I might see you dance. It is a sight for which I would gladly risk my entire kingdom. Through their antennae, I feel your dance's rhythm. Yes, I have sent many soldiers as close as I dared to the volcano of your anger. Many suffered the swift punishment of your broom. But I never wanted to frighten you. I never wanted to make you unhappy."

Rosa doesn't know what to say. Certainly, far in the back of her mind, she always knew that someone was watching her, appreciating her lonely skill with the wooden partner. (She even let the broom think he was the one in the lead.) Certainly, sometimes in the night, she had fantasized that these faithful rituals might bring her notice. This, however . . . this was far more than she had ever dreamed. Why, she wondered suddenly, had this monarch come to her now? What did he want?

"Señora, I now risk everything. I have revealed myself to you tonight in order to promise that my people will never trouble you again. The only thing I ask, what I humbly beg in return is simply this: one dance."

Ah, ha, thought Señora Rosa Villarosa. So this was it. And was it not understandable? Was it all for nothing that she had very nearly been chosen Corn Maiden in her youth?

Repressing any triumphant smirks or conceited head-tosses, Rosa draws herself up and, with another demure nod, extends her hand.

From behind the walls, the music swells. Trumpets and marimbas sound as the King gallantly skitters forward. Reverently, he enfolds her in four arms and they begin to sway.

"Oh!" she says as he moves her in ways that the broom never could. The many black hairs on his feelers transmit his excited sensitivity to her, and she comes alive, melting into one turn, flashing to the next.

"Ah," she sighs, closing her eyes to feel it all better.

Roaches skitter in from every corner of the room. In the blinding speed with which she whips around, they look like fairy dust.

There goes the box of Ritz crackers. There goes the toaster and all the bacon fat for the week. If she opened her eyes to see, would she even care? Shining like a comet, she shoots around, sparks around, pouts hair mouth legs flings around.

His chuckle is rough. His enclosing arms push a little sharper now. But he spins, spins, spins her, so it's all right. She won't think about what happens when it's over.

Her heart is fluttering. Her work is undone, but there's no one to see. No cares as to what the neighbors would say. Her future is forgotten and her back hurts a little, too. But, oh . . . It's so, so romantic.

Eddie

Since I have to be in this room for an hour and a half every day, with nothing to do for the last hour, I figure I may as well write my memoirs or whatever. Kind of like that book, *The Catcher in the Rye,* except this is real, and you wouldn't catch any pimps beating up on *my* ass.

We're supposed to be in here to learn how to read and write. It's part of some new literacy thing they're doing, supposedly to make us better people . . . to give us "an alternative to crime." Me and this other dude in here already know how to read and write. So for the first thirty minutes they wanted us to help the other guys with their stuff, but as you can imagine, the other guys didn't want our help. So now, I do whatever I want in this room, which isn't much. I wrote to my sister and my dad a few days ago, but they haven't answered. So now I'm writing this to kill time. I figure maybe it'll help people to see why I don't belong here.

First, let me go back to my childhood. I used to be a good kid. I had a normal family—a mom, a dad, a sister, a brother. We had a nice house. We were doing pretty good. I don't remember that part too well.

Then, after my mom left, things started to suck. This was when I was about five. We had to move. We lived in some apartments for a while, then we moved in with my grandma so she could take care of my little brother while my dad was at work. My messed-up uncle and his messed-up son moved in, too. Things were okay for a few years, until my dad lost his job and we had to get on welfare. Then, a few years after that, when I was around sixteen, my grandma died, and it was just us and my dad. But I already knew how to steal way before any of that.

I remember one time, when I was just a little kid, my mom had taken us to Eckerd's. She used to like to take us places and just look at stuff. This time, though, I saw a toy that I wanted. It was one of those little Play-Doh factories. I remember I asked my mom if I could have it and she said she didn't have any money, so I started to cry. She told me to be a big strong boy and not to cry. Then she put the toy in Jesse's diaper bag. I stopped crying. We kept on looking at stuff, and Tina, my sister, saw a little plastic necklace with a unicorn on it. She asked my mom if she could have it. My mom told her to be a big girl and not to whine. Then we just kept walking.

I'm not saying that one incident made me become a thief. I'm just telling you about my life. Sometimes I remember my mom would want stuff for us, but she wouldn't steal . . . she'd beg. Like, once, when she took us to the park. There was a guy loading up Mountain Dew in the vending machines. My mom went up to the guy and asked him for a six-pack, saying it was real hot. The guy told her she would have to wait and buy it from the machine. My mom started begging him to please give us a six-pack. She said we were poor and hadn't eaten all day. She pointed to us and said she didn't have any money to buy us food or clothes. The guy looked at us and then he gave my mom the sodas. I always thought that was weird when I remember it, because my dad made good money back then. I don't know why the Mountain Dew guy believed my mom. Now I've figured out that he probably just thought she was hot and was hoping she'd give him something back. But, anyway, all I know is it was a pretty humiliating experience, and, since then, I've always preferred stealing to begging.

It's time to go to the laundry room now, so I'll write some more later.

๛๛

I didn't start stealing hardcore until we got on welfare. Before that, it was just candy and toys and stuff. It was always easy because we look white like my mom, and everyone was always keeping their eyes on the all-Mexican kids instead of me. Me and Jesse used to get all kinds of stuff. Tina never wanted to, though. She had a real guilty conscience. It'd make her real nervous and she was always scared to get caught. In fact, she did get caught a few times. I remember one day during summer vacation, me and Jesse took her with us on our daily rounds. She was going to be our thief apprentice, like. We took her to Level One, the bakery. All she had to do was go in, pretend to look at stuff for a while, and then go out, grabbing a bag of chips from the rack by the door. Child's play. So what does she do? First she goes in all nervous, looking around in a real suspicious way. Me and Jesse were standing outside the door watching.

Then she takes forever, trying to work up her nerve. Then, real fast, she runs to the rack, grabs a bag of Funions, and turns to the door. That's when she slips on the greasy wood floor and falls on her knees. Everybody in the store looks to see what all the noise is. My sister is so humiliated, she just leaves the chips there on the floor and walks out with her jeans torn and her knee all bloody. Defeated. Me and Jesse cracked up. After that, when we went places, she would just point to what she wanted and I would get it for her.

By now you're probably thinking, "Man, this guy is a punk." But it's not like that. Let me explain. It's one thing for kids to steal candy. That's just natural. But after a while, they get old enough to know better. You know, old enough to know right from wrong. I mean . . . everybody knows it's wrong to steal from people, right? Like, if I were to go to someone's house and steal their stuff, that would be wrong. Or, like, I knew this one guy who stole money from a teacher's purse. She was a real nice teacher, too. She never hassled you when you were tardy or you didn't have your homework. She just marked you tardy or gave you a zero, and that was it. I always thought she was pretty cool. But this guy just stole from her purse. And all she had was ten bucks. So he was a real punk. You wouldn't catch me acting like that.

On the other hand, sometimes a person has to steal. Food, for instance. Everybody knows it's okay to steal food—as long as you're really starving and you steal it from a big store and not somebody's house or anything. And not from, like, a neighborhood store where the people running it only have that store and that's how they're making their living. I know that now. I mean, the 7-11 is one thing. But I stopped taking stuff from the bakery and the Vietnamese store. Those people were always cool with me.

Another example would be that it's okay to steal from Goodwill or the Salvation Army. One time I went to the Goodwill and saw this real nice Polo shirt. I wanted to get it, but it was $3.99. All I had was four bucks, and I still hadn't eaten. So I found another shirt that said $2.99, and I switched the tags. When I take it up there, the lady tells me, "I'm sorry, sir," (being, like, sarcastic), "but we can't sell this shirt. This tag has been tampered with." I told her could she just give it to me anyway, because there were a lot of shirts that said $2.99. She kept on saying no. She was being real shitty about it, too. I finally told her, "Damn, y'all get the shit for free. It's not like one dollar's gonna make a big

difference." She just turned around like she didn't hear me
and I walked out with the shirt in my hand. Fuck her. I figured she probably just wanted to keep it for her boyfriend or
something.

So, anyway, I guess my point is: under some circumstances it's okay to steal. But not from other poor people.
Because, I mean . . . if poor people start stealing from each
other, how can you trust anybody?

It was a little while before my grandma died that Tina
started working. Partly because we could use the money, and
partly, probably, to get out of the house. I know it was pretty crappy for her, living there, because she had to do most of
the cooking and cleaning and my dad was always yelling at
her when he got drunk. Sometimes he even slapped her
around a little. He was okay when he was sober . . . it was
just on the weekends that he drank and got all tripped-out on
Vietnam and stuff. But you could hardly blame him. He kept
trying to get jobs at new places, but they kept telling him he
was over-qualified. Then he had that job at the grocery store,
which sucked. So the weekend was his only time to relax.
Except, like I said, he didn't really relax too much.

Anyway, so my sister had gotten this job at the church.
She went after school and did typing and filing and some
cleaning up in the office. It was a pretty good job, consider-
ing that they probably didn't really need anyone to do that
stuff. But they liked my sister at the church, so I guess they
felt sorry for her. Plus, she knew how to type, and I don't
think the regular secretary did. Plus, she spoke more Spanish than the regular secretary spoke English, so that probably helped, too.

Meanwhile, we were all still going to school. I hated
school. Nothing but a bunch of punks. Me and Tina had been
in this "gifted and talented" program since second grade.
That meant we had to take the bus to schools on the other

side of town, while everyone else in the neighborhood got to walk. At first I liked it okay. That was when I was too young to know better. The year that I failed, they took me out of the gifted and talented program. I stayed at that junior high for a semester, in the regular program, until they could get me transferred out to our neighborhood school.

Man, I was glad when I got transferred. There was nothing but a bunch of rich fags and snobby bitches at that other place. All they did was look down on people. Like, I had this one friend named Gabriel. He was the smartest dude in the whole school. I'm not just saying that, he was. He always scored the highest on the tests they gave us. Plus he was real cool, too. Real funny. The only thing was, he was real poor. He only had this one pair of shoes, and they had holes. I could tell he got his stuff from Goodwill, because it was stuff I had seen there myself.

One week, he wore the same outfit three days in a row. I didn't say anything to him about it . . . you never know what somebody else is going through. But a bunch of the other kids started teasing him about it, saying he must have been retarded because he'd bought three of the same outfit. They wanted to know if it was his new school uniform. Gabriel was real cool about it; he just laughed it off. But they kept on. Besides being poor, Gabriel was real skinny and he had a limp, like one leg was longer than the other. So these guys started in on him about that, too, calling him Gimpy and shit. They all got around him and just kept messing with him, like a gang of punks. So Gabriel just told one of them, Scott Jenowski, something about how he was stupid. I can't remember what exactly he told him, but it was a real good put-down, and it pissed Scott off real bad and shut him up. So Gabriel turned around to go. But that punk Scott, he pushed Gabriel and made him fall, and him and all his friends started laughing. Man, that was just too much for

me. I went up to that asshole and punched him right in the
face. I mean hard, too. Busted his lip. He sure as hell wasn't
laughing after that. Then he hit me back, and one of his
friends jumped in, and I was just swinging and kicking as
hard as I could. I messed both those guys up bad. Then one
of the cafeteria monitors came and broke it up.

We all got suspended . . . even Gabriel. And the worst
part was, after that, I never really talked to him anymore
after that. I think he was too embarrassed. But, anyway, you
see what I mean about that school. It was like, if you weren't
rich, they treated you like crap. I couldn't hang with that.
Tina, though . . . she loved it. She hung out with all those
white girls. Then she went on with them to the gifted and talented high school. I think that's why she really got that job,
so she could buy nice clothes like her friends. Sometimes
she would even steal stuff from Foley's, but usually she was
too scared Anyway, me and Jesse got away from those people as soon as we could.

⇜⇝

When me and Jesse first went to Hogg Middle School, I
spent the first week beating the crap out of everyone who
called us *bolillos* and honkies and stuff. After that, it was cool.
That's where I made some of my best friends. There were six
of us: Elías, Chuy, Fat José, Skinny José, and Huicho. Plus
me. And Jesse. He was always tagging along. Sometimes it
got on my nerves, because Jesse could really be a punk . . . but
I figured, if I didn't show him how to act, who would?

Mostly we would just mess around. We'd skip class
about two or three times a week. Sometimes we'd walk
downtown or take the bus to the dollar movies and sneak in.
Sometimes we'd go to Chuy's dad's and listen to records
and maybe smoke a joint. The night time was best, though.
For some reason, there's more good stuff to do at night.

We'd go to the mall and scope out the girls. Then we'd go to the clubs on Richmond. Either we'd sneak in, or we'd just wait for the rich punks to come out so we could take their gold chains or whatever. A couple of times we went to concerts. Once in a while, Huicho would get a car and we'd cruise around at Memorial Park.

I remember this one time me and Chuy had gotten a ride to Westheimer and we were walking around seeing the sights. There were a bunch of hookers that night, and even a couple of transvestites. Right when we passed that restaurant called the Purple Buddha, this guy comes up to us. I could tell he was a fag and I guess he thought we were queer-baits or something. I was about to tell him to take off, but he got real close to us and whispered, "Help me."

He had this real weird look on his face, and for a second I thought maybe he was having a heart attack or something. "What's up, man?" I told him.

He said could we please help him. I asked him what he needed. He said, "I need you to choke me."

First I freaked out. Then I just laughed. Chuy laughed, too. We started to walk away, but the guy said, "Please! I need someone to choke me!" He grabbed Chuy's hand, and Chuy told him, "I'll choke your ass, man." He grabbed the guy's neck for real and started choking him. I was tripping out, but I was laughing, too. Chuy kept on until the guy turned red and stopped breathing. Then he let go and said, "There. Now quit fucking with us."

I expected the guy to run. But instead, he says thank you! He wiped the tears out of his eyes, reached into his pocket, and pulled out a twenty-dollar bill. He gave Chuy twenty bucks for choking him! Chuy tripped out. He just said, "Thanks, you fucking freak."

Then the guy looks at me all coy, and asks if I would choke him, too. I was like, man, for twenty bucks I'll choke

you and your mama. So I did it. And he was saying, "Harder."
And I did.

After he paid me, the guy asked if he could call us sometime. Chuy just kicked him in the balls and we took off.

☙

Couldn't write too much last time 'cause these two
dudes started having a fight in here. They're gone now. Then
today the warden came in to talk to us. But anyway, like I
was saying . . . Don't get me wrong. It's not that I hate fags.
As a matter of fact, there are some fags in our neighborhood
who are pretty cool. They've been trying to fix stuff up. I
don't mess with them. It's only when they mess with me that
I have to kick their asses.

Like there's this one who lives over in First Ward. Every
time you walk by, he says stuff to you. Not to me, though,
because I told him I don't play that shit. But I know this
dude named Danny. Danny would always say stuff back to
this old fag guy. Then, later on, I heard that Danny and a
couple of other dudes were going to the fag's house and letting him do stuff to them. You know . . . like giving them
head. Then the fag would give them beer and pills and stuff.
I mean, they did it for beer, man. All I know is, if Danny or
one of them ever tries to talk to me, I'll kick his ass.

Anyway. After I finished at Hogg, I went to Reagan.
That wasn't too bad because most of my friends (everybody
but Elías and Skinny José) passed to the ninth with me. In
fact, that was probably my best year in school. They let us
eat lunch outside. I got to take art, and our coach in gym was
pretty cool. Besides that, I skipped most of the time. But the
work was real easy, so I didn't fail that year. Mostly I just
had a good time. I even hooked up with this chick for a
while. Her name was Elizabeth. She was fine, too. I found
out later she was a slut, but it was okay while it lasted. Like

I said, it was a pretty cool year.

I was all happy that summer. I thought tenth grade was going to be cool, too. So, of course, that's when all the bad stuff happened.

Jesse had started hanging out with a little gang of punks he met at Hogg when I wasn't there. I mean, these people were total criminals. They would steal cars from their own neighborhoods, then just drive them around and wreck them. They even stole from their own families. Jesse started stealing records from Tina's room. Then, when she asked him about it, he'd just lie. I think they were on crack, too. They were always stealing money, or stealing something they could sell to get money. It's one thing to smoke weed, but only First Ward punks smoke crack. I know they were on some shit, because one time Kiki López came to our house looking for Jesse. Kiki didn't sell weed, but he sold everything else. So I figured either Jesse owed him money, or else he was dealing for him.

I tried to tell Jesse to cut his shit out. He just cussed me out. It was weird, because he used to always want to hang out with me and my friends, and then all of a sudden he was acting like he was too bad-ass for us. Like I said, I tried to talk to him about it. Then I tried beating the crap out of him. Nothing worked.

Like, this one time, me and him were walking downtown. For once, we were getting along okay. I remember we were talking about Bruce Lee. Then, all of a sudden, we saw my mom across the street from us. I grabbed Jesse's arm so I could pull him into this deli we were in front of. But he thought I was screwing around with him and he pushed me.

Then, I guess my mom saw us because she started coming across the street. Cars were honking at her and stuff. I started walking fast like I didn't see her, pulling Jesse with me. My mom was right behind us, like she was chasing us.

Finally she says, "Edward? Is that you, baby?"

It was too late to play it off anymore, so I just stopped and waited by this fountain for her to catch up. Jesse said, "C'mon, man," but it was too late and I had to just act cool while she walked up to us.

People were looking at my mom and at us. I told this one dude in a suit, "What the fuck are you staring at, man?" Then they stopped looking.

"Baby, I've been trying to find you," my mom says, all out of breath. Then she starts on her usual thing. She tells us how we have to come with her to New Mexico to get away from my dad, because he's secretly the Grand Dragon of the Ku Klux Klan and he's going to sell us into white slavery. She says she has a job waiting for her there as the manager of a hotel, and that me and Jesse and Tina can all have our own suites, as long as we work as the janitors. I told her okay, that it was a good plan.

Meanwhile, Jesse's cracking up. I give him a look to tell him to chill out, but he keeps laughing. Then my mom takes a torn-out magazine page from her bag and writes some guy's name on it, telling me to call this guy at the *Houston Chronicle* for bus fare when we're ready to go. I say okay. I take the paper and start to walk away.

But Jesse didn't walk away with me. He just stood there looking at her. Then he told her, "You are one fucked-up bitch, you know that?"

Man, you have no idea how humiliated I was. I was tripping out. My mom just kept tying up her trash bag like she didn't hear, and then she picked it up and walked away. And Jesse yelled at her, "Yeah, that's right, get the fuck out of here, you crazy bitch!"

I didn't want to make a bigger scene than it already was, so I just didn't say anything until we had walked all the way to the bayou. Then I told Jesse, "Man, you must have no snap at all. What the hell's wrong with you, talking to our mom like that?"

He said why did I care how he talked to her, since she was just a crazy bitch. He was really pissing me off. I tried to tell him that even if she was crazy, she couldn't help it and he shouldn't talk to her like that. He told me I was fucked in the head and to shut up. I grabbed him and told him not to walk off when I was telling him something. He pushed my hand off his arm, real hard.

That's when I just couldn't cope with it anymore and I hit him. We had a fight right there at the Sabine Street Bridge. We probably would have killed each other if it hadn't been for the cop car coming our way. We saw it, and Jesse jumped up and took off. So I just walked home real slow, looking at the sun go behind the buildings and wondering how I let Jesse turn out the way he did.

ࡋ✒ᠥ

Meanwhile, my dad had started getting drunk all the time. He had been fired from the grocery store after he got arrested for DWI and missed two days. So he just stayed at home and watched TV and drank beer. We all just tried to stay away from him. Jesse and me hung out all night, and Tina slept over at her friends' houses whenever she could.

The weekend after that stuff happened with Jesse, I was at the Utotem playing video games with Elías and Chuy. All of a sudden, I hear my dad saying, "There he is. There's my son, the neighborhood badass." I look up and see him with one of the local drunks, some guy everybody calls the Captain. I finished my game, entered my initials for the high score, and told my dad, "What's up?"

"Hey, bad-ass, why don't you buy your old man a beer?" He's already holding one in his hand, and I tell him that. He just turns to the Captain and says, "See? He's not only a bad-ass, he's a smart-ass, too. See what happens when you have kids?" He laughs. The Captain nods and laughs, too, not knowing what the hell my dad's talking about.

My dad keeps laughing, louder and louder, real phony, like he's going to die laughing. Then, suddenly, he stops laughing and gets this real pissed-off look on his face. He starts yelling then. "Do you see what happens when you BUST your ASS, trying to raise your children to be DECENT HUMAN BEINGS?" He throws his bottle of beer at a Corn-Nuts display, and it knocks stuff all over the place and breaks on the floor. "You search for the PERFECT WOMAN to plant your SEED into . . . trying to produce PERFECT, DECENT CHILDREN . . ." The Iranian guy comes out from behind the counter and starts waving his hands, telling us to leave. "And WHAT do you get? This . . . this PIECE of SHIT . . . this NEIGHBORHOOD BAD ASS . . ."

My friends are real cool. They just kept playing Galaga like nothing was happening. The Captain had gone out to the dumpster to hang with the other drunks there. The Iranian was getting really freaked out, so I told my dad I would buy him a beer and made him follow me out the door. He kept on yelling as he handed me his keys and got in the car. By the time we got home, he had chilled out a little and was just talking loud instead of yelling.

I started trying to get him in the house, but he stopped in the middle of the yard and pushed me away. "Get your fuck-ing hands off me!" he says. "I don't need help from a sorry piece of shit like you." I just stood there and didn't say any-thing. He kept on. "Do you know how ashamed of you I am? Do you know what you are? You're just a punk. A criminal. You're worthless. You're NOTHING." Then he starts with the laughing again. "Just another neighborhood bad-ass. Come on, bad-ass. Kick my ass. Why don't you kick your old man's ass? You know you want to." He raised his hands like he was a boxer. He took a swing. He fell forward and landed on his face in some old flowers my grandma had planted. I just left him there and started walking back to the store.

About two blocks down from our house, there's this really nice place, like a little mansion. It's one of those Victorian kinds of houses with all different colors of wood and a big porch and real big windows. It even has two little dog statues on the top of the steps. Real cool. Nobody lives there. It's supposed to be a historical landmark, just for show. I was walking by that house on the way to the store and I saw a pick up parked in front of it. Not one of those funky yellow or orange two-tones like everybody in the neighborhood drives . . . a real nice black Ford with custom paint, dual wheels, an extended cab and everything. I was wondering who would be on our street with a truck like that. I knew it wasn't one of the fags, because they always drive Saabs or Volkswagen bugs.

I was thinking that whoever it belonged to must have been stupid to leave it there like that, and then the engine started up. I couldn't see who was in it because the windows were tinted. But then the passenger door opened and a girl got out. It was my sister. I stopped where I was and took out a cigarette, being real casual. She leaned over to kiss whoever was in the driver's seat. I took a few steps closer and saw it was this faggot-ass white dude, probably from her school. Tina shut the door and went into the yard of the historical house. She stopped on the steps, turned around and waved bye. The guy honked the horn and took off, peeling out real loud just like a fucking punk.

I was halfway over there when Tina looked around and saw me. For a second she looked surprised, then she just looked casual like nothing had happened.

"What the fuck was that?" I told her. She said "What?" like she didn't know what I was talking about. I told her why

was she in that guy's truck and why did he drop her off here.
She said Josh was her friend, and he had taken her to dinner.
"Dinner my ass,"

I told her. "Then why were y'all parked here all that time?"

She got this snotty look on her face and told me she
didn't need me getting in her business. I told her she had
made it my business when she drove around the neighborhood acting like a slut for everybody to see.

She said I didn't have any right to talk to her like that
because I didn't know anything. She said I needed to follow
her example, to get off drugs and start doing better in school.
I told her to shut up, that at least I wasn't fucking some
white guy for money. She got all pissed off. She said for me
to shut up, that she was tired of lazy drug addicts telling her
what to do when she was the only one in the family who
wasn't a complete waste.

I told her "Fuck you, slut." Then I spit on her.

That made her seriously mad. She slapped me, but not
real hard because I saw it coming. Then I hit her. I just
couldn't stop myself. I didn't mean to do it hard, but I guess
I did because there was blood on her face when I took off. I
remember she was crying and yelling, "You stupid punk!
You broke my nose! You stupid fucking asshole!"

❧❧

After that, I lived with Chuy for a while at his dad's
place. His dad had gone to Mexico. I just needed to chill out
for a while. Really, I only spent the nights there. During the
day I walked around downtown and stuff. I liked to go to the
library because they had air conditioning and nice little
couches you could sit on while you looked at stuff. Sometimes I went to the Park because they had a lot of gourmet
stores and cappuccino places there that would give out free
samples. If I woke up early or stayed out real late, I would

go to the Seven-Eleven and get some of the donuts they were throwing out from the day before. On Wednesdays, if I was around Tranquility Park, I would go there and watch the old people play checkers and backgammon. They always had coffee and some donated cookies, and they were pretty cool about sharing.

One day I went back to my neighborhood, just to see if anything was going on. I was walking by old Mr. Santos's house. It was one of those houses that old Mexican people always live in, painted pink or peach with flowers and Virgin Mary's all over the place. Mr. Santos was sitting there on the porch in one of his white iron chairs. I looked at him and nodded, and he told me, *"M'ijo, ven."*

For a second I tripped out. Mr. Santos had never talked to me before. I had never even heard him talk to anybody. I was thinking maybe he was a fag and he was getting me confused with Danny or somebody. But I went through his gate and up to the steps to see what he wanted.

"Hijo, you see that grass?" He pointed to his yard. "I got a lawn mower in the back. I'll give you ten dollars to mow that grass."

He only had the kind of mower that you push, with no gas, but that was cool. His yard was real small, so it was easy. After I finished, he told me I could sit on the porch and rest. I thought, aw, man, now the faggot stuff's going to start. But it didn't. I just sat there and Mr. Santos started telling me stuff. Not lecturing me, like you would expect, but just stuff about his life and everything. I figured he was just bored living there all by himself and wanted to talk to somebody. So I chilled out for a while and listened. He was kind of religious, but I didn't mind. All in all, it wasn't too bad.

৵৵

The next day I was walking around that area again.

Across the street from Mr. Santos's, Mrs. López was in her yard with her walker. She called out in a little crackly voice, "*M'ijo* . . . could you come here, please?" So I went.

She said she saw how I did such a good job on Mr. Santos's yard, and could I please do her yard, too. I said okay. I had to go borrow the mower from Mr. Santos. Her lawn was even smaller than his, and while I mowed it she just scooted around on her walker, scoping out her plants and stuff. When I was finished, she told me, "God bless you, *m'ijo*." She only had five dollars, but that was cool.

I was walking around, wondering what I should spend my money on. I was thinking maybe I could get some ham and cheese from the Vietnamese store and take it to the house. Maybe my dad would want some, too.

All of a sudden, this guy I know, Crazy Tony, comes up to me saying "Hey, Eddie, man, got some tickets here. I'll sell you two Metallica tickets for a hundred each."

I told him to get his lying ass away from me. He said okay, he'd sell them for fifty. I just laughed. He started begging, saying he really needed the money. So I played along, saying, "All right, man, but all I got is fifteen bucks." He looked at me for a long time, like he was thinking about it. He was blinking real hard and the side of his mouth kept going up like it does sometimes. Finally he said, "Okay, man, but hurry up before I change my mind."

I took the money out of my pocket because I wanted to see what he had that he thought was two Metallica tickets. I figured I'd wait until the last minute and then tell him I wanted Air Supply tickets instead. He reached in his pocket and took out . . . Damn! I thought. He took out two Metallica tickets! And not old stubs, either. Real tickets, for the show the next night. I grabbed them, gave him the money, told him thanks, and took off. I was going to go find Chuy and tell him so he could go with me to the concert.

But on the way to Chuy's dad's, I saw Jesse and two of his friends going down Washington. I was going to just play it off and not say anything, but he told me "What's up," so I stopped.

He was just talking to me real normal, like that stuff with our mom hadn't happened the other day. I could tell he felt bad about it. I did, too. So all of a sudden I told him that I had two tickets to Metallica and asked him if he wanted to go.

ঌ⋙ঌ

There isn't a lot to tell after that. We went to the concert. Fifteen minutes into the show, Jesse tried to yank a chain off this white chick's neck. She started cussing him out and scratching him. He hit her. Then her boyfriend and two of his friends jumped in. What else could I do but jump too? They would have beat the shit out of Jesse. When the security guards got there, everybody had taken off except me and the chick's boyfriend. I was the only one who got arrested.

I had some prior arrests so I thought they'd try me as an adult. But since I was young and it was mostly just minor stuff, they ended up putting me here.

It's not too bad. I'm one of the oldest ones, so nobody messes with me. I only have a few months to go. I figure, with Jesse's record, they would have had to give him the electric chair if they'd caught him. Not really . . . I'm just kidding about that. But he definitely would have gotten a lot longer sentence than I did.

So maybe it's better this way. I know you're probably thinking that I should be real pissed off at him. At first I was. But now I've had a lot of time to think about it, and I realize that he's just a kid. A lot of fucked-up shit happened to him in his life, and he just wasn't old enough to cope with it. So that's why he's the way he is. He can't help it.

Anyway. I got a letter from my dad the other day. He got

a new job at some kind of organization. He says he likes it there. It sounds like he's doing okay. He said Tina got married to some guy from the church. I figure that's why she hasn't written. She probably doesn't want this guy to know she has a brother in jail. I can understand that, so I won't mess it up for her. My dad didn't say anything about Jesse, so I'm taking that to mean he's okay, too. I guess they're all doing good.

See, like I said . . . I've had a lot of time to think in here. I figure, our family just had some bad luck. We were going through a phase or whatever, and I happened to get the worst part of the deal. But that's all right. Stuff like that happens to people all the time. In a few months I'll be out of here, and everything will go back to normal, like it used to be.

Meanwhile, I'm just going to kick back for a while. I may as well, right? I've been needing a vacation, anyway.

Alexandra and Me

*I*know it's evil, but we stole the midget. Sorry—the little person. Or is she a dwarf? All I know for sure is that it was Alexandra's idea. Sure, I said that I wanted to carry the tiny woman around by the waist, holding her high and far from my body like a trophy or a doll, taking her higher and lower on the balls of my feet. But it was Alexandra who wanted to steal her, to finger her tiny barrettes and rings. To question her. To ignore her answers and drape her in the Indian fabric we bought on Interstate 59. And I went along with it. Alexandra is awfully gorgeous in her constant anger, and I can't deny her anything.

"Please . . . why are you doing this to me?" the tiny woman cries. Her name was Holly, I think.

"Shut up. I've been here for months. Let me out, you bitches!" rasps the bus driver I tied up in the corner, actually only six weeks before. But, no, it wasn't because I was angry. Only lonely and a bit disappointed by life, and dripping more than usual inside from that time of the month. Who doesn't want to possess a tiny, swarthy man with haunted eyes? He smiled at me, so I took him home and paid for him to get high. When he couldn't keep it up, he started to slap me around. I know I should have just let him go, but the way his hair fell into his eyes made me feel tender, and I decided to keep him, instead. Renting this house with the basement was the best plan we ever had. So what if the flood had given it a bit of mildew? Now it was even more of a testament to our bargain-shopping prowess.

I sigh and walk over to caress my bus driver's cheekbone and neck, to press a leftover piece of pizza to his soft, sharp lips. "You fat, fucking whores," he moans as he chews, tears rolling over the pockmarks. "You big devil bitches from hell!" I kiss his ear, but neither of us is cheered, and I put the pizza back on the paper plate.

"Save it for the midget," says Alexandra. "I want her hair to grow." The man cries, the midget cries, and Alexandra doesn't care. She's often angry, but I don't get scared. We've both been hurt. Broken. Used. I understand her. She's me, but turned inside out. She doles out the harsh justice that I, guilt ridden save for myself.

Together, we're strong. We listen to each other, protect each other, lie for each other, believe in each other. When we're together, the skinny sluts don't snicker until well out of earshot. The sticky men think twice before reaching out with their tentacles. Everyone else just stares. Look at the fat chicks. The big girls. The amazons. Angry and sad but cackling like thunder—shaped by epic cruelty—aren't we exactly the same as every goddess you've ever heard of? When we're smiling at someone's expense, distracted for a moment from our own inner workings, you can almost see the pretty potentials we used to be.

Alexandra works her jaw, deaf to the whining as she unconsciously pinches the midget's ear. Her eyes flash yellow in the light of the TV, which is playing a sappy teen romance. I go to her, close my own eyes, and lean in for the kiss that has eluded me so far. But then the cat cries out upstairs. Alexandra lumbers up quickly to tend to it. "I'm coming, Booboo! Mommy's coming!"

I follow, softly closing the padded door behind me. It's

okay. Later she'll want to brush and style *my* hair. I'll finish hammering out the necklace I've been making her. We'll eat cheap pastries and plot and laugh. We'll watch a sappy teen romance and, when it's over, we'll cry ourselves to sleep, together in the dark.

Tina

The radiator had made it too warm to cover herself with a sheet, but Tina did anyway. She felt it chafe her clammy skin, but pulled it higher, up to her mouth, as she heard the crackling again. This time it came from the bag of soda cans. She could tell because the crackle was metallic and rustling at the same time. It sent little needles of fear and disgust into the back of her neck and down through her spine, all the way to her toes, which she pulled up further under the sheet. She lay there and listened.

There. Another one. This time skittering across a stack of newspaper. She grimaced, thinking that it must have been something big for her to hear it on the paper. Not a roach, then . . . a rat.

It was Sunday night, the night before school would re-open after the Christmas holidays. It was the first time she had slept in her own room in two weeks. She thought wistfully of the night before, which she'd spent at her friend's house in a nice, queen-sized bed. She had many friends, and had managed to spend every night of the vacation somewhere else. And now it was over. She peered into the dark corners of her room. Was that another one?

Before Christmas, she had survived by working as late as Mrs. Vargas would let her, then hanging out with the more nocturnal of the neighborhood kids, until she was so tired that she would get home and immediately fall asleep, deaf to the noises. Then, of course, on the weekends she slept over at Jennifer's, Adriana's, or Melissa's. Now that the winter had finally kicked in, it was too cold to be on the street, unless she wanted to try to keep warm with the thuggiest of the thugs. And it seemed that this winter was worse, vermin-wise, than ever before.

Summer vacation was the best. She could sleep some-where else every night, sometimes even with Mrs. Vargas's family at the marina. She didn't have to be at work until noon, so even if she felt she was starting to wear out her wel-comes, she could just stay up all night, walking through the church grounds or the park. Sometimes she ordered a pizza from the phone booth across the street. Sometimes she met up with one of her peers, maybe even one with a car, and so had companionship and conversation for the night. She remembered, with a mixture of pleasure and regret, the pre-vious summer when she'd been "going" with Manuel. The nights had never seemed long enough then. She would return to her house when the sun rose, and sleep peacefully while the rats and roaches hid from the light of the day.

A loud, skittering crackle, this time combined with a squeak, erupted two feet behind her and frightened Tina out of her memories. She hopped off the couch and ran out into the hallway, stubbing her little toe on a box of old newspa-pers on the way.

The house where she lived had, many years before, been a six-suite apartment building. Each suite had one tiny liv-ing room/bedroom with a walk-in closet and a radiator, a bathroom with a footed tub, and a long, narrow kitchen with a porcelain sink and real wood cabinets in either peach or pale green. The floors were wood. The walls were all real sheetrock, except in the hall, where there was also wood wainscoting and paneling. The house itself was built of many shades of brown brick. With extensive renovations, it might have made a nice office building, especially being so close to downtown. Her father had bought it for his mother in better days, and being a landlady had given Grandma a nice little income. Then, when Daddy had lost his job and his wife, Grandma had turned out all the tenants (most of whom were illegal immigrants, used to relocating on short notice), so that her son and his three children could move in. One of Tina's uncles had already been living there on and off, rent-free, and other family members moved in shortly after they had.

Over the years and through several half-hearted attempts at remodeling, the apartments still retained their little brass numbers over each door. She ran back to Number 6 now and knocked.

"Daddy! Daddy! Wake up! Open the door!"

After several minutes of trying to make herself heard over his snores, she realized it probably wasn't a good idea to wake her father after he'd spent the afternoon drinking. She looked across to Number 5. Her brother Eddie was out, his door locked. Her youngest brother normally shared that room, but he had been in juvenile for the past month. Number 3 was locked as well. Her cousin Rudy would be at the bars until morning. She walked past her own door and the two kitchens whose walls had been torn down, to the front of the house. Number 2 was a room she avoided at all times. Uncle Juanito lived there, and he was a dirty old man.

She turned and walked through the open doorway of Number 1.

Although she loved her grandmother, Tina knew better than to expect sympathy from her. But maybe, just this once, Grandma would let her sleep on the sofa.

"Grandma . . . are you awake?" Tina's eyes adjusted, and she saw the sugar-and-spice-colored mass of hair, illuminated by the reading lamp the old woman was using to do a crossword puzzle.

"Of course I'm awake. How can I sleep with you yelling like that? Are you trying to wake the whole house up?" This was said without any negative inflection, though, and Tina went on.

"Grandma, can I sleep in here tonight?"

"Why? What's wrong with your own room?"

"I think there's a rat in there."

"So?"

As if to amplify her grandmother's point, a mouse ran across the room, going right over the old woman's toe. Time girl gasped. Was Grandma becoming senile? The affected foot flexed and un-flexed, as if in reply. No . . . she just didn't care.

"If you can't sleep, why don't you stay up and clean your room? That's what I do. Or you could sweep the hallway. Or you could . . ." Her next suggestion was interrupted by the sound of the front door opening. "There's your brother." She called out, "Lock the door behind you, *m'ijo.*" Tina hurried into the hall.

"Eddie, can I sleep in your room?" Tina whispered, because her father didn't like her sleeping in Eddie's room. It didn't occur to her that he couldn't hear her asking.

"What, you're tripping out on the rats again, Big Sis?" His breath smelled of Wild Turkey. "I told you, you should make 'em your pets. That's what poor people gotta do. Just get you some little ribbons, then get you a net . . ."

Ignoring his advice, Tina stayed close to him until he unlocked his door.

Everyone in the house, except Grandma, locked his door. They all felt that they had something to protect from the others. Eddie's something was his stash. His room contained the same brown tweed couch as the others', and also the same twin-sized bed that had originally been in the apartment. The shabbiness of those two pieces had been somewhat disguised, however, by a vast array of stolen goods that made the room look like a sheik's tent. The couch and bed were draped with red and gold throws—some velvet, some just velour. There was what appeared to be a zebra-skin rug on the floor. Whereas the windows in Tina's room had old, pink-and-green flowered sheets stapled across them, Eddie's windows were adorned with bamboo blinds. Every surface in his room was crowded with Buddhas, dragons, or naked ladies . . . some from the Goodwill, and some from the best stores in the Galleria. The exception was the long shelf above his stereo, which supported his prized collection of empty liquor bottles.

Eddie graciously offered the bed to Tina, and she lay down, finally ready to sleep. Then Eddie went to the stereo, put on his Anthrax cassette at full volume, and turned off the light.

"Um, Eddie . . ."

"It helps me sleep."

ॐ-ॐ

The next night, Tina crossed the threshold of Number 4, dressed for bed and still damp from her bath. (Her bathroom didn't have running water, so she used her grandmother's tub.) Almost as soon as her head touched the flattened pillow, she heard the crackle. Damn, she thought, I can't take this anymore. She wished she had remembered to ask Eddie for the key to his room the night before.

She got up, went to a corner of the room, and picked up the broken-off piece of broomstick that she kept there for protection. (One New Year's Eve, they had a party, and one of the cousins . . .) It occurred to her that maybe a little music would help her sleep the way it did for Eddie. She went to the nightstand and turned on the little radio. She set it to the classic rock station and turned it down to barely audible. They were playing Elton John. He wasn't Tina's favorite, but she thought something good might come on next. She set the broomstick down by the bed, and lay down. Sure enough, the next song was a good one. "Deacon Blue," by Steely Dan. She closed her eyes and listened. She felt herself starting to relax. Then she let herself slip into a favorite fantasy.

She was in her own apartment, far away—maybe in New York. The walls were white. There was a white sofa and a pale gray carpet. She was lying on the carpet, listening to her stereo, her Steely Dan record. Maybe there was . . . no, she was alone. It was clean and peaceful. Maybe she was a college student. . . .

Crackle.

Yeah, right. With her recent grades, that really was a fantasy. And since this was already her senior year, it was too late to think about college now. She shifted on the bed.

Okay. Maybe she was a writer. A famous writer who wrote about life in the barrio . . . whose books were read world-wide . . .

Crackle.

Sure. As if anyone would want to read about her crappy life. As if anyone would believe it. Tina rolled onto her other side. The only way she would ever get out of this place would be to meet someone. Someone who could take her away. Some rich, white guy—like the ones she saw at the mall sometimes. Like the one she had seen in Foley's last week with the cool haircut and the green eyes . . .

Tina rolled her eyes under their lids. Yeah, the one with the girlfriend with the long, blonde hair. There was no use even dreaming about a guy like that. The best she could hope for was one of the guys at the church. Like Robert, who had taken her to the last youth-group dance. Or Mario, who she had been with the weekend before. He wasn't so bad. What would it be like to be his wife? She considered it. No, Robert was better. He wasn't as pushy, and he drank less. He had a nice car, since he worked at the body shop with his dad. Yeah, Robert was okay . . .

She started to drift off to sleep, imagining herself living with Robert in a little pink house in the Heights. There was a garden, and a back yard, and running water, and a baby, and an exterminator . . .

Crackle, crackle. Skitter, crackle.

Tina shrieked and jumped off the bed. She grabbed her broomstick, ran to the bag of cans and beat it savagely. There! Take that, you bastards! There were squeaks and scrabbling sounds.

She beat the stack of newspapers with the stick. There, you sons of bitches.

She hit everything in the room. Tears were streaming down her face. She swung the stick hard, hitting the doors and the walls, knocking things off the little table and dresser. She hit the radio, and it fell down with a crash, breaking into several pieces.

"Go to hell, all of you! I hate you all!"

She sank back down to the bed. She closed her eyes and promised silently to herself: I am not sleeping here tomorrow.

Then she lay back down and, clutching her stick, fell asleep.

Love and Humanoids

*O*nce there was a woman who was very valuable without even knowing it. In a nearby galaxy, unbeknownst to her, was an alien race of human-sized ants who enjoyed the sexual excretions of humanoid women as a culinary delicacy. They keep tiny, insect-sized humanoid women on ranches in the 40-longitude range of their planet. For most of the ant people, the sugary syrup made from the excretions of these tiny humanoid women is enough. They purchase the syrup at their grocery stores and pour it over their breakfast aphids in the morning.

For rich ant people, there's a special syrup made from the lubricants of real human women. Ant merchants send ships to Earth at night in order to cultivate the valuable substance from dirty panties. It can be dried into crystals and served like caviar. It's a very profitable business, and the ant people conduct it nearly undetectably, unlike other importers in search of other things, who leave hazy memories of anal probes wherever they go.

One night, a ship funded by a very successful ant corporation finds what it's looking for, which is this special human woman whose secretions are superior and highly desirable in every way. The ship's team hones in on the particular wavelengths this woman emits and abducts her. Her panties are not enough.

᠙᠊ᢦᡩ

Stephanie washes the dishes slowly, her hands rubbing weak circles on each filthy plate. She's well fed. She's not missing any limbs. But a tear runs down her cheek. She wipes her hand across her face. It leaves a trail of soap, suds in her hair. She turns off the water with a sigh.

She walks to the living room, picks up the remote control, points it at the TV. Puts it down again without turning anything on. Looks at the clock but doesn't see the numbers. The light coming from the window shows that it's too late for her boyfriend to be out, but too early for anyone to go to bed.

She goes to bed and, after a few hours of twisting under the sheets, starts the first of her habitually unpleasant dreams.

"Bobby, I love you. Why do you keep leaving me?" she calls to the man in the spacesuit.

"Baby . . . your body's dirty and your highlights were bought for cheap," he says through his mirrored mask.

She runs toward him, even while the brightness behind his head is making her cry. He's pulled farther and farther away. She's running so hard, her feet leave the ground. But the light's too bright and she can't see him anymore.

᠙᠊ᢦᡩ

The ant people connect the subject to a device that will hold her safe in unconscious stasis while they prepare the programs that will create a virtual, alternate reality in the subject's mind.

"Goddess, I wish we could start harvesting its juices right now. I need all the bonus checks I can get."

"If we force it to excrete now, its primitive hormonal responses will negatively affect the first batch. Or, worse, its psychological framework will destabilize and all our work will be useless."

"I know, boss . . . I know, ma'am."

"Then quit complaining and get back to work."

The team works according to its carefully designed plan. The first psuedo-reality program they feed to the subject is a quick resolution of her current circumstances.

෩෧

Stephanie jerks awake and grabs the phone on the night-stand within the first ring.

"Miss Luna?"

"Yes?"

"I'm sorry . . . I'm calling to tell you that your boyfriend's been in a car accident."

"What?"

"I'm sorry, but he didn't make it, Miss Luna."

"What? Oh, my God . . ." Stephanie's hand grips the receiver tightly.

"I'm sorry, but apparently he was distracted by the fella-tio being performed on him by his coworker Angie, who was also in the car."

"What? Oh, my God!"

"I'm sorry."

෩෧

"Get me one fifty cc's of sugar, stat."

"Yes, ma'am."

The ensign carefully attaches the glucose bag to the subject's IV. The team then sets its timer for a year-long recovery period. For the next two weeks, they watch movies and play a game similar to ping-pong in the ship's lounge. They take turns monitoring the subject—maintaining its hydration and sugar levels throughout hundreds of perceived crying jags and pastry binges. The ship meanders from outpost to outpost, its robot fingers carefully collecting the distilled panty crotches sent into space by billions of hard-working minions all over the Earth.

ॐ∼త

Stephanie blows her nose and throws the wadded tissue toward the small pile of empty cupcake wrappers. She changes the channel again.

"Oh, Brad . . . take me, you hot, sensitive pirate!"

Nothing but more soft-core porn. Have the cable channels finally managed to broaden the definition of prime time?

This time, Stephanie doesn't turn off the television. The actors seem to get better looking every night. She's riveted to the screen.

Later, in bed, her hands are riveted to her sides as the trashy movie replays in fast motion in her mind. Finally, guilt- and sweat-ridden, she lets the hands furiously touch her body under the sheets until she's completely exhausted and able to sleep.

ॐ∼త

"Gimme the swab, Crych! Let me try it!"

"Hold on, hold on . . ." Ensign Crych pulls the swab away, but Flsyk snatches it out of his claw, then rubs his feeler along the tip.

"Oh, my copulating Goddess! This is *excellent*. This is the mother-copulating…"

"Ensign Flsyk. Please." The captain, as always, has appeared without warning.

"Sorry, boss." Flsyk surrenders the swab.

"Mm. This *is* excellent. Ensign Crych, awaken Dr. Xotcd from stasis. It's time to begin."

Once the program designer and xenopsychologist Dr. Xotcd is awake and able to watch his subject's real, live reactions to stimuli, results come in much more quickly. The doctor doesn't run out of volunteers to test them by running their tongues slowly and deliriously over the swabs. His teammates give each other high-fives. (Actually, they're high ones or high thousands, depending on whether you count the one limb or the thousands of sensitive hairs across its tip.) They congratulate themselves on how wealthy they're going to be. This subject's juices are that good—like poppy nectar or cricket-people glands, but without the messy side effects or the jail time. Dr. Xotcd reads his data and rasps his antennae, but the others ignore him.

"Accelerate the programs, Dr. Xotcd."

"Yes, ma'am."

∂◦∽

Stephanie pulls at the halter neck of the black dress. Even though she must have lost tons of weight—she had to have, in order to fit into Elena's dress—she feels uncomfortable here, tonight. Like it's all some sort of joke. Like, any minute from now, everyone's going to put down their martinis to point at her and laugh.

"There you are. God, you look hot tonight."

Stephanie flinches away from the hand brushing her bare shoulder. She turns and sees him—Brad Rockley, the handsomest, trendiest man in the room.

Why is he talking to her?

"What's wrong, Stephanie? Show me your beautiful eyes and tell me what I can do to make you smile."

She tries to laugh lightly, but it comes out more like a gagging sound.

"What—did Elena get you to do this?"

"Get me to do what? Darling, please . . . just let me kiss

you once . . ."

Stephanie gasps and stumbles back, down the stairs, away from him. He reaches for her blindly, his eyes closed in an imitation of passion. That bitch Elena. Stephanie *knew* she shouldn't have trusted her. And she knew she looked fat in this dress!

Arms crossed over her exposed flesh, Stephanie runs to the street to hail a cab.

こ~✧

Dr. Xotcd's antennae rub together softly, creating a rasping sound.

"This is what I was afraid of. All along, the subject has shown a slightly irregular response . . . irrational levels of guilt- or fear-induced enzymes . . . This is something I've come across in my studies, but I'll need time to research . . ."

The captain's antennae flicker impatiently.

"Will these enzymes affect the results? I want to have something to show the CEQ when we dock next week."

"Well . . . not to an extent that . . . They might affect the chemical composition, but probably not so that it's noticeable to the palate. But they could create within the subject a . . ."

"Change the scenario. Give me results."

"But . . . Yes, ma'am."

こ~✧

Stephanie pulls at the black leather collar around her neck. Brad, clad in a silk kimono, walks into the room with a riding crop in his hand.

"Hello again, Stephanie."

Stephanie doesn't answer. Her eyes are wide, her arms and legs bound.

"You know what I'm going to do to you, don't you?"

Still no answer. Brad kneels down so that his mouth is level with her ear. He whispers into it.

"You *want* me to do this to you, don't you?"

Stephanie emits a quiet sob that could mean yes or no. Brad's lips touch her ear as he whispers again.

"Let me put it this way: I'm going to do this to you whether you want it or not. But you do want it, don't you? Say it."

She lets out a slightly louder sob and nods her head.

కపోళ

Back at the home office, Dr. Xotcd shakes his head at the monitors. This particular program is distasteful to him. However, he's been charged to produce results, and the subject's thoughts—conscious and sub—have shown that this is the quickest way to do it. And, besides, he must remember to keep his personal feelings out of his projects. The captain's note on his last review flickers through his mind. "Hindered by tendency to anthropomorphize his subjects."

The subject's body flushes and flinches under the electrodes. Her essence flows into the collectors at an unprecedented rate. Xotcd's antennae rasp as he goes to his console to absorb the most recently translated Earth media: web sites, movies, romance novels. He'll stay up all night writing code for bonds and restraints, submission and surrender. He only has two months to set the permanent program before it's time to fly back to Earth for the next project.

కపోళ

The salty wind lashes at Stephanie's hair and the frayed edges of her bodice. The worn, wooden plank hits her in the small of the back as she backs away from the pirate captain. He and his mates leer at her hungrily.

"Aye, lass, there's the plank at your back. Are you going to walk it, or stop your struggling and play nice with us?"

Her tears are whipped away toward the sea.

"But . . . but . . . Do you even *want* to play with me?" she says. "I'm not very pretty. My thighs . . . they're so fat."

The pirate captain laughs a wicked laugh. "Missy, my men here have been at sea for a long time. You're as good-looking as anything they can remember."

Stephanie looks at him from under her lashes, still uncertain.

"I get second turn with the wench, after Captain Brad!" the First Mate yells. A fight breaks out among some of the others as the captain rips away what's left of Stephanie's corset with his bare hands.

‽∞‽

"Hurry up, Flsyk. I don't want to be late." Ensign Crych paces near the door of the anteroom.

"Just a second . . . how's my tie look?"

"What do you care? You're not gonna get anywhere near the queen."

"That's what you think. After I do get my chance with her, she's gonna remember my scent. I might even get a promotion out of it," Ensign Flsyk says to his teammate and to his own reflection. "Dream on, beetlesucker. If you want a promotion so bad, why don't you try servicing the captain?"

"Are you kidding me? I tried it two months ago. She nearly broke my thorax!"

"Whoa. Yeah, I heard that about her . . ." The hairs on Crych's limbs ripple.

"Hey, Dr. Xot, what about you?" Flsyk yells into the lab. "You going to the Queen Fest?"

The doctor looks up from the print-out he's been reading at the subject's table. Is it Queen's Festival Week already?

"Aw, he can't hear you, Flsyk. He's busy with *his* queen."

"His queen . . . Yeah! Good one, Crych!"

The ensigns clack their mandibles loudly as they leave the anteroom. Dr. Xotcd goes back to his work.

࿐

Stephanie steps into the bath. The slave girl sprinkles the water with jasmine oil, the sheik's favorite. He's requested that his newest harem girl, the exotically fair and plump Stephanie, be ready within the hour.

"Stephanie?" the slave girl whispers.

"What is it, Xora?"

"Are you . . . are you happy here?"

Stephanie considers the question for a moment.

"Why, Xora? Are you thinking of escaping?"

Xora considers this question in her turn, then nods.

"Well . . . I hope you make it, because I can see how you'd probably hate being here. I'll help you if I can. But . . . I don't think I can leave with you. See . . . I don't have anywhere to go, really. Plus, I don't know . . . Call me an idiot if you want, but I don't really mind this life. I mean, it's not so bad. It could be worse. Sometimes I think the sheik actually kind of cares about me. You know?"

࿐

Dr. Xotcd remembers the humanoid farm he received as a hatchday gift from his parents one summer. He enjoyed putting little bits of sugar into the tunnels and watching the tiny brown and beige mammals overcoming barriers to find the food and carry it to their homes. Working within this single human subject's mind is like that, but much more enthralling. This isn't as real as a humanoid farm, because the barriers are all abstractions. And, yet, at the same time, it's much more real than a colony of tiny animals could ever be.

This is what he's thinking when his teammates troop into the lab.

"Bonus check, Dr. Xotcd. Congratulations," says the captain as she hands him an envelope.

Ensigns Crych and Flsyk are already tearing theirs open.

"Yes. Goddess, YES!" says Flsyk upon seeing the amount.

"Hey, look . . . there's a memo on the next project," says Crych. "Scouts just got back from Earth. Our team is assigned to go pick up ten subjects. Whoa. That's a lot. Wonder what they're for? Not for Project Special Blend? I thought they were getting ready to synthesize this subject's juices?" He waves a feeler in the direction of the human who's been a permanent fixture in the lab since they got back from the last trip.

Flsyk scans his memo.

"Hey, maybe . . . maybe it's for that new sports thing I heard about . . ."

"I have no such memo in my envelope," Dr. Xotcd says to their captain. "Mine was accidentally omitted."

"Actually, Doctor, that was no accident," she says. "Your services won't be necessary on this project. Dr. Thrstyk will accompany the team, instead."

Thrstyk? That old-colony braggart? Dr. Xotcd waits until his haphazard emotions subside before speaking.

"What will my assignment be in the meantime?"

"Maintain the current course. I will meet with you before our departure, in two weeks, for a final briefing."

"Yes, ma'am."

Xotcd keeps his antennae curved neutrally. He doesn't want the captain to suspect that he'd relish this opportunity to delve further into his studies with the human.

☞☜

"Baby, I love the way your eyes shine when I whip you," Stephanie's latest master says, dropping the whip and grasping her hair in his hands.

"Oh, Raul! I knew you felt the same way I did! Can we get out of the dungeon tonight? Just snuggle on the couch and watch TV? I'm so glad you love me like I love you. I've felt this way so many times, but it's never been real before . . . never like this. I'm going to make you so happy. We'll be happy together…"

Raul lets go of her hair. He takes a step back and fiddles with his executioner's mask for a moment.

"Uh . . . What? Hold on. Uh . . . hold on, slave. I'll be right back."

Raul looks around the dungeon for a moment, then, suddenly, drops his whip and bolts up the stairs.

Stephanie stares at him. Her ropes hold her firmly in place, keeping her from reacting physically to the shock.

"What?" she whispers. "What did I do?"

෧⊶෨

Dr. Xotcd examines the monitors, then keys in a slight modulation to his code.

෧⊶෨

Passed on to a new master, Stephanie's bitter but not yet totally pessimistic. Martin strides into the room, a cat-o-nine tails in his fist.

"On your knees, slut. Bow your head when your master speaks!"

"Yes, Master."

"That's right."

After holding her head down for what feels like the appropriate amount of time, Stephanie lifts it again and says the words she's been rehearsing in her mind all afternoon.

"Master Martin, I just want you to know that I have every intention of doing my part in this relationship. I know that you're going to treat me badly. But, also, I know why you're going to do it. You've never had a slave that really appreciated and supported your needs as a dom. I know that you're just like me . . . you just want to be loved, and no one you've ever known has loved you the way you deserve. Until now. I'm willing to love you, Master Martin. And I'm going to accept your mistreatment, because I know it's just your way of showing that you want to love me, too."

Stephanie bows her head again. Master Martin is speechless for quite a while. Then:

"What the hell are you talking about, you crazy bitch? What the . . . Get the hell out of my dungeon!"

"What? But . . . I thought . . ." says Stephanie.

"I said get out!"

The tears well in her eyes again as she stumbles away.

Șȡ

Stricter masters don't work. More exotic scenes and sex don't work. Dr. Xotcd even tries writing the code so that the men actually do "love" the subject. But those scenarios don't result in the secretions that pay for his research.

He shuffles his notes nervously. He's not looking forward to his meeting with the captain. Although she's never warm by any means, her cold distance is infinitely preferable to her actual displeasure. It's unfortunate that the project couldn't continue optimally until she departed for the new assignment.

The captain enters the conference room, her antennae click, click, clicking.

"What happened to that last batch, Dr. Xotcd? I thought the enzyme issues had been resolved."

"Yes, ma'am, they were, but new issues have arisen. The subject is no longer achieving maximum levels of pleasure with the submissive scenarios. Her emotional responses have modulated out of the range of the programs, and her dissatisfaction apparently taints the results."

"This is very annoying."

"Ma'am . . . if you would permit me, I have a suggestion."

"What is it?"

"My research has indicated that the subject's reactions to date are most likely the result of traumatic incidents during her developmental phase. We have the technology to go back and erase the trauma from the subject's memory. If I could have a few months to identify and realign—"

"Look, Xotcd, we don't have time for this." The captain's feelers rasp against each other once, twice. "The subject is dissatisfied by the submissive role, you say?"

"That is correct, ma'am."

Several facets of the captain's eyes gleam.

"Then I'd say it's time for a switch."

☙❧

Stephanie tugs at the chain attached to the young man's collar. He scurries on his knees across the carpet to the kitchen to bring her a drink. Stephanie puts her feet up and lets her riding crop rest on her knees. Now *this* is the life.

"Madam . . . the new slave is ready. She's waiting for you in the dungeon."

"Thank you, slave," Stephanie says, standing and swatting at him affectionately with the stiffened leather braid. She laughs aloud as she walks down the stairs. Her experience has taught her well, and now she's reaping the rewards. Her clients pay plenty to be spanked, degraded, and reamed with a strap-on. Life is going to be easy from now on.

She opens the dungeon door. A plump, young blonde kneels on the stone floor, all done up in black vinyl.

"Mistress Stephanie, please accept me as your slave. I've been a bad, bad girl!"

❧

The lab technicians report that the levels of tasty acids and pheromones in the latest batch are through the roof. The company has recovered its Special Blend, with a higher market value than ever. Dr. Xotcd is relieved. And then . . .

❧

Stephanie falls in love with the blonde slave and lets her run away.

❧

Xotcd tries slaves of different types, desperate to keep the project on track. Smaller, darker males do well for a while, until the subject's frustratingly inevitable sympathy for her subjects kicks in and the scenarios are derailed. Older, paler male slaves have the interesting effect of inciting anger. The subject unleashes hitherto unseen violence against them, kicking and shouting. But she doesn't climax from this. She does, however, release perspiration that turns out to be quite effective as a stain remover. The formula is synthesized and sold for a tidy profit.

Although the company's chemists persist, they remain unable to synthesize the subject's sexual fluids. The exact make-up is indefinable, available only from the subject herself, under increasingly specialized circumstances. Dr. Xotcd is under pressure. Pressure to perform.

His brief attempt at turning the subject back into a slave is quickly aborted when it unleashes her most violent reaction. Researchers, designers, programmers, and xenobiologists gather for grave meetings. Profits can't drop. The CEQ won't have it.

New human subjects with similar chemical builds have been taken from Earth, but the methods don't work on them at all. For some reason, these subjects resist the alternate-reality mental programming. They reject it entirely, and the company is forced to restore them to stasis lest their mentalities collapse.

Worst of all, People for the Ethical Treatment of Humanoids has gotten wind of the company's methods of profit. In a flurry of tersely worded secret memos, Dr. Xotcd and his subject, along with the failed Special Blend Project abductees, are sent away to another lab, hidden under one of the company's caterpillar-milking facilities.

Emotionally taxed and uncertain of his future, Dr. Xotcd decides to lay low for a while. He sets a basic background program—food, water, shelter—for his subject. He leaves the subject to her own devices while he updates his resume and puts out feelers for new opportunities, just in case.

෧෨෨

Burned out on her old way of life, Stephanie decides to live off her savings for a month or so while figuring out what to do next. She spends her time in her apartment poring over the want ads. Stares at the ceiling. Eats. She's gaining weight again. She doesn't really care. She has more important things to worry about.

"Wanted: coffee shop waitress," an ad says one day when she's almost out of money.

Customer service isn't unlike many things she's done before. It's full of degradation, humiliation, and kissing ass. Stephanie becomes good at her new job.

૭~૭

The lack of contact from Xotcd's bosses makes him nervous, at first. Then, he reads about the success of the company's latest project. Rich clients pay handsomely for the most vicious, violent imported human males to compete in their sports arenas. His former teammates have been back from Earth for a while now and are preparing to go back and import more subjects from the planet's military forces. The company's other scientists have been able to successfully alter the subjects' testosterone, increasing their lust for blood. Human-fighting has become the latest craze. The company's resources and watchful eye are completely focused on it.

The waning human lubricant trade is temporarily forgotten. The pressure's off Xotcd and the paychecks still come. He decides to dedicate himself fully to his current research. He imagines that he might publish or even win a prize, even while he accepts the more likely fact that no one will really care.

૭~૭

"Hey, baby. How about a little sugar with that cream?"

Stephanie ignores the customer's request for affection. She hasn't felt like dating lately.

"Oh, Brad—at first our biting banter and violent passion thrilled me, but lately I've been hungry for something else. Please, darling—just hold me!"

Stephanie turns off the TV. All the shows have become so boring and crass.

She goes to the used bookstore and trades in her romances for the books that were considered racy decades ago. She goes to the flea market and acquires a free kitten to keep her company in her apartment late at night.

Right before she goes to sleep, she doesn't think about movie stars or her boss' muscular arms. She thinks about mundane things, like dishes and bills. It's boring. The boringness puts her safely to sleep, where she dreams of bills and dishes. It's almost like she's dreamed too much in the last few years, and now she has to fill her dreamtime with other things.

శ్రీ

Again, this is like the tiny humanoid farm—something to care about. Xotcd goes into the program module and leaves surprises for his subject to find—attractive mates, opportunities to excel at her chosen livelihood, little bits of cake. Some treats she takes, and some she ignores as she industriously scurries through her life.

It's like an imported holographic drama, but with Xotcd himself as the director. And he can accelerate it. Make the story, with its potential happy ending, tell itself faster.

శ్రీ

"I'm crazy . . . Crazy for feeling so lonely . . ."

Stephanie sometimes goes out with her friends to the karaoke bar after work and, when she's had enough to drink, takes the stage and makes them cheer with her sexy or swaggering imitations of divas and rock stars.

Naturally, the coffee shop's open mic night was her own idea, enthusiastically embraced by the owner and the clientele. But, so far, she's too nervous to perform there herself without any artificial background music as a safety net.

Months pass in a blur. Finally, one night, encouraged by her new friends, Stephanie stands at the microphone and falteringly sings a song she learned as a child, fingers stumbling across grade-school chords on the borrowed guitar. This isn't the kind of performing she's done before, where everything out of her lips is a stale cliché spoken for somebody else's pleasure. Here she expresses her real feelings, and the audience actually listens. Without riding crops in their hands. Without ropes holding anybody down.

The nervousness twisting her stomach is quickly replaced by a surge of excitement. Her voice rises, then whispers, then just flows. The song's over and everyone applauds. She feels a brand new feeling—something she'll have to examine tonight, when she's alone.

☙❧

The Company's periodic self-review survey reaches Xotcd's hidden lab.

1. List your recent contributions to the success of the Company.
2. Describe your value as a member of your team.
3. Detail your ideas for bringing profit to the Company in the near future.

The survey remains unanswered on his console. Any of his peers, in Xotcd's place, would take advantage of the opportunity to pander their way back into the colony's good graces. Back into the rank and file. Back into the common mind.

Instead, Xotcd rushes to fit together the pieces of a profitless puzzle. He's used to being alone.

☙❧

"Xena, guess what?"
"Meow?"
Stephanie tells her cat the good news. After a year of hard work, she's been promoted to day-shift manager at the coffee shop. This means more money and maybe a nicer apartment for them both.

She's too excited to spend the evening reading or revising her song lyrics. Impulsively, she decides to see if her luck will hold by going to the talent contest at a local club tonight. Normally, she wouldn't be brave enough to compete against others, but what does she have to lose?

Not only does she win, but she's engaged for a monthly gig. The audience really likes her song. A couple of people ask if she has CD for sale. She hasn't ever recorded one. Maybe she should look into it.

The next day Stephanie takes her prize money and, for the first time ever, completely splurges on things she wants but doesn't need. It's okay. She can afford it. She deserves it.

That night, she celebrates the results of her hard work by taking a long, luxurious bath and then massaging herself with expensive new lotion. Feeling languorous and warm, she slips into bed and drowsily fantasizes about the future. She caresses herself softly until, for the first time in a long time, her hand slips down under the waistband of her pajamas . . .

&~&

Xotcd is surprised, then pleased, then immediately apprehensive. He wonders if he's required to report this unexpected development to his new supervisor.

There's no need. His supervisor has set her electro-antenna to automatically vibrate when the sensors record the subject producing valuable fluids. Before Xotcd can formulate a plan, she and her ensigns swarm into his lab.

"Rslv, take a swab and run the test. Quickly."

"Yes, ma'am."

"Good work, Dr. Xotcd. We'll take it from here." The supervisor folds four of her arms across her thorax and waits for the results.

The latest lubricant, while certainly normal, is no Special Blend. The team sets up residence in the compound surrounding the lab. Two whole weeks pass before the subject produces again on her own.

"This is ridiculous. Dr. Xotcd, introduce stronger stimuli," says the supervisor, who is like his former captain, but younger and even colder.

Xotcd does as he's told. He codes burly men, gorgeous women, sexy scenes. The subject rejects them all—eludes them as if they're hallucinations or dreams. She has become completely resistant to passive acceptance of her circumstances.

ॐ॰ॐ

"So, Stephanie . . . recording your first demo! Congratulations!"

"Thanks."

"And how's everything going at the coffee shop?"

"Great—busy. I've been hiring new waiters. We've gotten so many more customers since we started the open mic nights and art exhibits. It's crazy. But good crazy."

"And . . . ?"

"And what?"

"Don't mess with me, Stephanie! What about this new guy? What's his name—Tad? Rad?"

"Robert. And we're just friends."

"Aw, come on."

"No, seriously, Elena. I'm taking this extra slow. I don't need anything to mess up my good luck."

"You mean your hard work. God, Stephanie, I'm so happy for you. You've come so far since . . . Well, since…"

"Since I got out of my old life."

"Yeah. I'm really excited for you . . . Can't wait to see what you do next."

♾

"What do we do next, Ma'am?"

"Nothing, Ensign Rslv. All of our efforts have failed. The CEQ says it's time to jettison the project."

"So . . . terminate the subject?"

Xotcd is horrified.

"No, Ensign, NOT terminate the subject," says the supervisor. "Haven't you been reading the news? People for the Ethical Treatment of Humanoids has been tunneling deep into Company business. We can't so much as test shell-shine on humans without it showing up on the nine o'clock holos."

"So . . . ?"

"So we return all the Project Special Blend humans to their *natural habitat.*" The supervisor's voice crackles with annoyance. She turns her antennae in Xotcd's direction. "Doctor, you will, of course, remove all the evidence."

♾

Xotcd suddenly, vividly experiences the memory of his mother dumping the humanoid farm and all its contents onto the sand pile behind their home. A few of the tiny creatures had escaped their confinement and gotten into the pantry. They'd made her angry. Xotcd cried.

"But, Mommy, I take care of them! They're my friends!"

"Nonsense, Xotcd. It's time you started playing outside, with the other children in our colony."

But he never did.

The weekend before the human females are to be removed, the doctor works overtime. First, he erases the inferior subjects' memories back to the point of abduction, as he's been instructed to do.

Next, he worries about what to do with *his* subject. What

are his options? He could erase her memory back to the point of abduction, but that would erase all the advancements made during their project.

He could erase only the unconstructive scenarios, leaving the subject with the memories of her own progress. But that progress would be incongruous with her situation once she was found by Earth authorities.

Finally, in a desperate frenzy, he realizes what he has to do.

∂∾⊰

"Stephanie . . ."

"Xora! Oh, my God. What are you doing here? I haven't seen you since . . . That's right—you escaped, right? God, that was such a long time ago . . . I can barely remember..."

"Stephanie, listen. I have something to tell you. This is going to sound strange, but I don't have a lot of time, so please listen . . ."

∂∾⊰

Xotcd restores all the subject's memories, from beginning to end, erased scenarios and all. Even the routinely repressed instances of the subject waking up in the lab and discovering the electrodes and sensors attached to her body. He tries to code the unfolding of the truth in the most optimal way possible, so as not to shock her into mental instability.

∂∾⊰

"Oh, my God. Oh, my *God.*"

"I know. I know. I'm so sorry, Stephanie. I'm so sorry you had to find out about everything—that none of it's been real."

"Then . . . If none of it's real, then what about you? What

are you? Are you real, or part of the program?"

"I'm . . . I'm a friend."

❧

Xotcd works throughout the two nights—eighty-six hours straight—and then is forced to let the export team take over. He remembers the bag of sugar he emptied onto the sand pile so long ago, when no one was watching. Now, just as then, he'll never know if it was enough.

❧

"Miss Luna? Can you hear me, Miss Luna?"

"Yes, I can hear you." Stephanie is groggy and sore. She sits up and focuses on the paramedic who's reading her name from the ID in her wallet. All around, other women are being roused from their sleep in the middle of a scorched cornfield.

"Where am I?" she hears them mutter. "What happened?"

Good questions. Where are they? What *did* happen?

Stephanie thinks back. Her mind stretches back, past the last long hours of dreamless sleep, past the lifetimes of the last few months.

"Miss Luna, are you okay?"

Stephanie lies back on the grass and sees the stars.

"Yeah," she says.

She *is* okay, isn't she? In fact, she's feeling pretty good. And everything's going to be great.

Additional APP titles by women

Crimson Moon
A Brown Angel Mystery
Lucha Corpi
March 31, 2004, 224 pages, Trade Paperback
ISBN 1-55885-421-5, $12.95

The Child of Exile: A Poetry Memoir
Carolina Hospital
March 31, 2004, 96 pages, Trade Paperback
ISBN 1-55885-411-8, $11.95

Princess Papaya
Himilce Novas
September 30, 2004, 240 pages, Trade Paper-
back, ISBN 1-55885-436-3, $14.95

Upside Down and Backwards /
De cabeza y al revés
Diane Gonzales Bertrand
Translation by Karina Hernandez
October 31, 2004, 64 pages, Trade Paperback,
ISBN 1-55885-408-8, $9.95, Ages 8-12

The Eighth Continent and Other Stories
Alba Ambert
1997, 160 pages, Trade Paperback
ISBN 1-55885-217-4, $12.95

A Perfect Silence
Alba Ambert
1995, 199 pages, Clothbound
ISBN 1-55885-125-9, WAS $19.95, NOW $9.95

Black Widow's Wardrobe
Lucha Corpi
1999, 208 pages, Trade Paperback
ISBN 1-55885-288-3, $12.95

Cactus Blood
Lucha Corpi
1995, 249 pages, Clothbound
ISBN 1-55885-134-8, was $18.95, now $9.50

Eulogy for a Brown Angel
A Mystery Novel
Lucha Corpi
2002, 192 pages, Trade Paperback
ISBN 1-55885-356-1, $12.95

Down Garrapata Road
Anne Estevis
2003, 128 pages, Trade Paperback
ISBN 1-55885-397-9, $12.95

Intaglio: A Novel in Six Stories
Roberta Fernández
1990, 160 pages, Trade Paperback
ISBN 1-55885-016-3, $9.50

Call No Man Master
Tina Juárez
1995, 334 pages, Clothbound
ISBN 1-55885-124-0, WAS $22.95, NOW
$11.50

South Wind Come
Tina Juárez
1998, 384 pages, Trade Paperback
ISBN 1-55885-231-X, $14.95

The Day of the Moon
Graciela Limón
1999, 240 pages, Trade Paperback
ISBN 1-55885-274-3, $12.95

Erased Faces
Graciela Limón
2001, 272 pages, Trade Paperback
ISBN 1-55885-342-1, $14.95

In Search of Bernabé
Graciela Limón
1993, 168 pages, Trade Paperback
ISBN 1-55885-073-2, $10.95

The Memories of Ana Calderón
Graciela Limón
2001, 300 pages, Trade Paperback
ISBN 1-55885-355-3, $12.95

Song of the Hummingbird
Graciela Limón
1996, 224 pages, Trade Paperback
ISBN 1-55885-091-0, $12.95

A Matter of Pride and Other Stories
Nicholasa Mohr
1997, 164 pages
Clothbound, ISBN 1-55885-163-1, $19.95
Trade Paperback, ISBN 1-55885-177-1, $11.95

Rituals of Survival: A Woman's Portfolio
Nicholasa Mohr
1985, 158 pages, Trade Paperback
ISBN 0-934770-39-5, $11.95

African Passions and Other Stories
Beatriz Rivera
1995, 168 pages, Trade Paperback
ISBN 1-55885-135-6, $9.95

Midnight Sandwiches at the Mariposa Express
Beatriz Rivera
1997, 184 pages, Trade Paperback
ISBN 1-55885-216-6, $11.95

Playing with Light
Beatriz Rivera
2000, 256 pages, Trade Paperback
ISBN 1-55885-310-3, $12.95

The Moths and Other Stories
Helena María Viramontes
1995 (Second Edition), 200 pages
Trade Paperback, ISBN 1-55885-138-0, $11.95

Women Don't Need to Write
Raquel Puig Zaldívar
1998, 352 pages, Trade Paperback
ISBN 1-55885-257-3, $13.95

In Other Words: Literature by Latinas of the United States
Edited by Roberta Fernández
1994, 592 pages, Trade Paperback
ISBN 1-55885-110-0, $20.95

Memoir of a Visionary
Antonia Pantoja
With a Foreword by Henry A. J. Ramos
2002, 384 Pages, Trade Paperback
ISBN 1-55885-385-5, $14.95

From the Cables of Genocide
Poems on Love and Hunger
Lorna Dee Cervantes
1991, 78 pages, Trade Paperback
ISBN 1-55885-033-3, $7.00

Terms of Survival
Judith Ortiz Cofer
1995 (Second Edition), 64 pages
Trade Paperback, ISBN 1-55885-079-1, $7.00

Palabras de mediodía/Noon Words
Lucha Corpi
Translations by Catherine Rodríguez-Nieto
2001, 208 pages, Trade Paperback
ISBN 1-55885-322-7, $12.95

How to Undress a Cop
Sarah Cortez
2000, 80 pages, Trade Paperback
ISBN 1-55885-301-4, $9.95

La Llorona on the Longfellow Bridge
Poetry y Otras Movidas
Alicia Gaspar de Alba
2003, 128 pages, Trade Paperback
ISBN 1-55885-399-5, $11.95

Shadows & Supposes
Gloria Vando
2002, 112 pages, Trade Paperback
ISBN 1-55885-360-X, $11.95

I Used to be a Superwoman
Gloria L. Velásquez
1997, 124 pages, Trade Paperback
ISBN 1-55885-191-7, $8.95

Thirty an' Seen a Lot
Evangelina Vigil-Piñón
1982, 72 pages, Trade Paperback
ISBN 0-934770-13-1, $7.00

Shattering the Myth
Plays by Hispanic Women
Selected by Denise Chávez
Edited by Linda Feyder
1992, 256 pages, Trade Paperback
ISBN 1-55885-041-4, $16.95

Beautiful Señoritas and Other Plays
Dolores Prida; Edited by Judith Weiss
1991, 180 pages, Trade Paperback
ISBN 1-55885-026-0, $12.95